True Stories of Real MOWGLIS and other Wild Children

True Stories of Real MOWGLIS and other Wild Children

Vikas Khatri

Publishers
Pustak Mahal®

J-3/16 , Daryaganj, New Delhi-110002
☎ 23276539, 23272783, 23272784 • *Fax:* 011-23260518
E-mail: info@pustakmahal.com • *Website:* www.pustakmahal.com

Sales Centre

- 10-B, Netaji Subhash Marg, Daryaganj, New Delhi-110002
  ☎ 23268292, 23268293, 23279900 • *Fax:* 011-23280567
  E-mail: rapidexdelhi@indiatimes.com
- 6686, Khari Baoli, Delhi-110006
  ☎ 23944314, 23911979

Branches

Bengaluru: ☎ 080-22234025 • *Telefax:* 080-22240209
E-mail: pustak@airtelmail.in • pustak@sancharnet.in
Mumbai: ☎ 022-22010941, 022-22053387
E-mail: rapidex@bom5.vsnl.net.in
Patna: ☎ 0612-3294193 • *Telefax:* 0612-2302719
E-mail: rapidexptn@rediffmail.com
Hyderabad: *Telefax:* 040-24737290
E-mail: pustakmahalhyd@yahoo.co.in

ISBN 978-81-223-1352-9

Edition: 2012

Printed at : Param Offsetters, Okhla, Delhi

Introduction

We all know the backdrop of Rudyard Kipling's "*The Jungle Book*": The young boy Mowgli is raised by wolves in the wild, but eventually is reunited with his human counterparts and taught the ways of man.

Amazing fact or urban legend? Do "feral children" exist? Can a child really be raised by wild animals? You'd be surprised by the number of documented cases that tend to support this premise: Small boys and girls raised by wolves, monkeys, bears and even gazelles – but who were not quite able to adjust back into modern society.

According to the studies there are nearly 70 documented cases of children being raised in the wild. Starting as early as 250A.D. with the 3-year-old roman boy Aegisthus – who apparently was raised by goats, all the way up to 2004 with the seven-year-old Russian child Andrei Tolstyk – who was found living with a pack of dogs, and by all accounts was recognized as the leader of the pack.

A surprising number of feral children have been documented in India and researchers feel it's easy to see why. Mothers would typically set their children down while they tended to work in the fields, only to have infants snatched up by wandering wolves and leopards. More often than not, the infant offered an easy meal, but this was not always the case.

The question remains: does a wild animal have the maternal instincts to raise a small child? There are documented cases of lions "adopting" small calves and other animals to make up for the loss of a cub. Cannot the same be done with a small infant? Who knows for sure?

Researchers tend to be more taken with the efforts (or lack of) involved in trying to re-indoctrinate these feral children back into society. In most cases, the efforts have been for naught.

Perhaps the Reverend J.A.L. Singh had it right when he wrote in his diary, "….I often wonder if the right thing to do would have been to leave these children in the wild where I found them…."

Information and Observations on Feral Children

Many wild children were extraordinarily fast quadrupedal runners – almost 'superhuman'. We might recall that Atalanta, the bear-suckled heroine of Greek myth, was the most swift-footed of mortals. When first captured, Memmie Le Blanc moved with "a sort of flying gallop" and could out-run game; and the Saharan gazelle-boy was clocked at 7mph faster than the best Olympic sprinter.

A facility for tree-climbing was another common trait. Peter (1724), Memmie, Victor and the Ugandan John Sesebunya were all agile arborialists; the last three were cornered up trees before their capture. The wolf-child of Overdyke in Holland, abandoned during the Napoleonic wars, climbed trees with wonderful agility to get eggs and birds, which he devoured raw. 'Tarzancito', the wild boy of El Salvador (1935) slept in trees to avoid predators.

A number of ferals were hirsute, including Jean de Liège (17th cent), the second Lithuanian bear-child (1669), the Kranenburg girl (1717), the wild boy of Kronstadt (fl.1784), the second Hasunpur wolf-child (1843), the Shajampur child (1898), and the Naini Tal bear-child (1914). A young man caught in woods near Riga, Latvia, in November 1936 was allegedly "covered in long thick hair".

"Over time all my senses were heightened – my vision, my hearing, even my sense of smell," wrote Misha Defonseca, the

Jewish orphan who wandered through Nazi-occupied Europe. "That hypersensitivity stayed with me for a very long time after I left the forest".

Feral senses were often more acute than those of socialised humans. Kaspar Hauser and many of the Indian wolf-children, including the Midnapore girls, could see well in the dark. Jean de Liège could recognise his warden by smell from a distance; Kamala could smell meat from one end of the orphanage garden – a compound of three and a half acres – to the other; and many wild children sniffed at objects in the way that cats and dogs do. Victor of Aveyron, the first Sultanpur child (1847), Kamala and Amala had an unusually sharp sense of hearing.

Many wild children had a keen ear for music. Peter was delighted by music, and would clap and sing. Memmie was a perfect mimic of songbirds such as the nightingale. The Overdyke boy named each bird by imitating its cry. A naked youth aged about 15, caught in woods near Uzitza, Yugoslavia, in 1934, could mimic animals and birds as well as run amazingly fast. The Turkish bear-girl responded to music, sometimes bursting into wild, unintelligible songs. John Sesebunya sings in a choir.

Another phenomenon is the wild children's insensitivity to extremes of temperature, a characteristic shared with desert nomad and gypsy children. This was seen in the Irish sheep-boy, Victor, the Kronstadt boy, the first Sultanpur child, the Midnapore girls, and the Saharan gazelle-boy. The latter was seen to grab a handful of hot embers and hold them for some time without apparent pain, while Victor took potatoes out of a pot of boiling water. At least eight ferals angrily tore off any clothing they were dressed in.

Hardly any of them learnt to laugh or smile and their libidos seemed stunted. Kaspar confused dreams with reality and spoke of himself in the third person. Neither Victor nor Kaspar could recognise their reflections in a mirror; the Turkish bear-girl would sit for hours in her room gazing at herself in a mirror. Auger observed the gazelle-boy looking at his reflection in a pool of water as if it were a stranger.

Skepticism

Many academics regarded the whole phenomenon of feral children with scepticism. Most of the children never learnt to speak, while those that did could recall very little of their wild existence. Similarly, the circumstances of their discovery were by their nature anecdotal, taking place far from habitation and often depending on the testimony of a solitary witness. Many accounts of feral children have been embroidered with fantastic details, inviting academic disdain. Dismissing testimony as superstition and folklore became commonplace in 19th century science, to the detriment of folk wisdom and forteana.

■ ■

Contents

Children Raised by the Wolves

Children Raised by the Leopards and Jackals

Children Raised by the Bears

Children Raised by the Apes

Children Raised by the Gazelles

Children Raised by the Goats, Sheeps and Cows

Children Raised by the Dogs

Children Raised by the Birds

Mysterious Wild Children

Children Raised by the Wolves

1. The Wolf Boy of Hesse

Confused by the Mists of Time

All the stories of the boys of Hesse and Wetterau are contradictory, confused, and frequently contain errors. The date of 1344 sometimes becomes 1544, and even 1744, in later commentaries, and the number of children varies from one to three. Sources include Dresserus, Camerarius, an unknown monk, and various others. Some of these sources are cited and quoted in Wolf Children and Feral Man by Singh and Zingg.

How Many Boys?

The reports are possibly referring to two wolf boys, one found in 1341 and one in 1344, or one in 1341 and a further two in 1344. Since the reports are so confused, these could all be the same boy: or it could be that the accounts we have available to us today have mixed the details of two or more different boys.

The Wolf-boy of Hesse

In the first case, that of the wolf-boy of Hesse, there are various accounts that might be about different boys. In some versions, a boy of 7 found in 1341 was cared for by monks but died soon after; a second boy, found in 1344 aged around 12 was possibly taken to the landgrave Henry of Hesse after capture. When staying in Henry's castle, the wolf-boy of Hesse behaved in a wild fashion, running around on all fours.

Because he didn't like normal food (and, presumably, because they failed to provide him with the raw meat to which he would have been accustomed), he also died soon after. However, this second boy sounds suspiciously like a confusion between the first and the third...

The Wolf-Boy of Wetterau

This is a summary of what Camerarius has to say about the third boy, the wolf-boy of Wetterau of 1344. Note the similarities with the (second) wolf-boy of Hesse; the major difference being that this chap lived to the age of 80.

A boy aged three was found near Echzel, in the forest of Hardt, in Bavaria, by which time he was about 12. He walked on all fours and was so loved by the wolves that they fed him with the choicest morsels of their prey, and they exercised him until he was able to run and jump with them. They (the wolves) took great care of his well-being, digging a pit to protect him at night and covering him with leaves. They lay around him to protect him from the cold.

After capture, he finished up in the court of the landgrave where he was looked after by servants, and was called Henry. He is quoted as saying that if it were up to him, he'd rather return to be among wolves than live with men.

2. The Wolf Boy of the Ardennes

Alexander Ross

Alexander Ross, in Arcana Microcosmi, (London, 1652, Tho. Newcomb, Printer) gives us this brief description of the Ardenne Wolf Boy:

"...a childe that was carried away in the Forest of Ardenne by Wolves, and nourished by them. This child having conversed with them divers years, was at last apprehended, but could neither speak nor walk upright, nor eat any thing except raw flesh, till by a new education among other children, his bestial nature was quite abolished."

Source

Ross gives the reference Divers Lecons, by Louys Guyon. Zingg gives for the same child the reference Schediasma de hominum inter ferus educatorum statu naturali solitario, Hannover, 1730, by Koenig, Henricus Conradus.

3. Wolf Boy of Kronstadt

This is an extract from Wolf Children and Feral Man by Singh and Zingg.

Here you have information about the wild boy who was found in the Siebenburgen-Wallachischen border [Romania] and was brought to Kronstadt [now Brasov], where in 1784 he was still alive. How the poor boy was saved from the forests... I cannot tell. However one must preserve the facts, as they are, in the sad gallery of pictures of this kind.

This unfortunate youth was of the male sex and was of medium size. He had an extremely wild glance. His eyes lay deep in his head, and rolled around in a wild fashion. His forehead was strangely bent inwards, and his hair of ash-gray colour grew out short and rough. He had heavy brown eyebrows, which projected out far over his eyes, and a small flat-pressed nose. His neck appeared puffy, and at the windpipe he appeared goitrous. His mouth stood somewhat out when he held it half open as he generally did since he breathed through his mouth. His tongue was almost motionless, and his cheeks appeared more hollow than full, and, like his face, were covered with a dirty yellowish skin. On the first glance at this face, from which a wildness and a sort of animal-being shone forth, one felt that it belonged to no rational creature... The other parts of the wild boy's body, especially the back and the chest were very hairy; the muscles on his arms and legs were stronger and more visible than on ordinary people. The hands were marked with callouses (which

supposedly were caused by different uses), and the skin of the hands was dirty yellow and thick throughout, as his face was. On the finger he had very long nails; and on the elbows and knees, he had knobby hardenings. The toes were longer than ordinary. He walked erect, but a little heavily. It seemed as if he would throw himself from one foot to the other. He carried his head and chest forward... He walked bare-footed and did not like shoes on his feet. He was completely lacking in speech, even in the slightest articulations of sounds. The sounds which he uttered were gibberish murmuring, which he would give when his guard drove him ahead of him. This murmuring was increased to a howling when he saw woods or even a tree. He seemed to express the wish for his accustomed abode; for once when he was in my room from which a mountain could be seen, the sight of the trees caused him to howl wretchedly... When I saw him the first time, he had no sense of possession. Probably it was his complete unfamiliarity with his new condition, and the longing for his earlier life in the wilds, which he displayed when he saw a garden or a wood. Similarly I explain why, at the beginning, he showed not the slightest emotion at the sight of women. When I saw him again after three years thus apathy and disrespect had disappeared. As soon as he saw a woman, he broke out into violent cries of joy, and tried to express his awakened desires also through gestures... Yet he showed anger and unwillingness when he was hungry and thirsty; and in that case would have very much liked to attack man, though on occasions he would do no harm to men or animals. Aside from the original human body which usually causes a pitiful impression in this state of wildness, and aside from walking erect, one missed in him all the characteristic traits through which human beings are distinguished from the animals; it was rather a much more pitiful sight to see how this helpless creature would waddle around in front of his keeper growling and glaring wildly, and longing for the presence of animals of prey, insensible to everything which appeared before him. In order to control this wild urge, as soon as he came near to the gates of the city, and approached the gardens and woods, they used to tie him up in the beginning. He had to be accompanied by several persons, because he would have forced himself free and would have run away to his former dwelling. In the beginning his food consisted only of all kinds of tree leaves, grass, roots, and raw meat. Only very slowly did he accustom himself to cooked food; and, according to the saying of the person who took care of him, a whole year passed before he learned to eat cooked food; when very obviously his animal wildness diminished.

I am unable to say how old he was. Outwardly he could have been from twenty-three to twenty-five years old. When I saw him again after three years, I still found him speechless, though changed very obviously in many other respects. His face still expressed something animal-like but had become softer... The desire for food, of which he now liked all kinds (particularly legumes), he would show by intelligible sounds. He showed his visible contentment when one brought him something to eat, and sometimes he would use a spoon. He had gotten used to wear shoes and other clothes; but he was careless about how much they were torn. Slowly he was able to find a way to his house without a leader; the only work for which he could be used consisted of giving him a water jug which he would fill at the well and bring to the house. This was the only service which he could perform for his guardian. He also knew how to provide himself with food by diligently visiting the houses where people had given him food. The instinct of imitation was shown on many occasions; but nothing made a permanent impression on him. Even if he imitated a thing several times, he soon forgot it again, except the custom which had to do with his natural needs, such as eating, drinking, sleeping, etc., and everything which had connection with these. He found his home in the evening, and at noon, the house where he expected food, led only by his habits. He never learned to know the value of money. He did accept it but only with the intention of playing with it, and he did not care when he lost it again. Chiefly he was in every respect like a child whose capacities had begun to develop, only with this difference that he was unable to speak and could not make any progress in that regard. He showed his likeness with a child in the fact that he would gape at everything which one showed him; but, with the same lack of concentration, he would change his glance from the old objects to new ones. If one showed him a mirror he would look behind it for the image before him. But he was completely indifferent when he did not find it, and would allow the mirror to get out of his range of vision. The tunes from musical instruments seemed to interest him, but it was a very slight interest which did not leave any impression. When I led him in front of the piano in my room, he listened to the tunes with an apparent pleasure, but did not dare to touch the keys. He showed great fear when I tried to force him to do so. Since 1784, the year he left Kronstadt, I never had a chance to receive any more reports about him.

4. The Hasunpur Wolf Boy

This account of the Husanpur Wolf Boy is taken from *A Journey Through the Kingdom of Oude* by Major-General Sir W. H. Sleeman (1788-1856): a distinguished officer, whose career in India extended over a period of forty years was born in 1788. He held the appointment of Resident at Lucknow from 1849 to 1856. During this period his letters and diary show his unwearied efforts to arrive at the best information on all points with regard to Oude. He had profoundly studied the Indian character in its different races, and was deservedly much beloved by them for his earnest desire to promote their welfare. In 1844 he published *Rambles and Recollections of an Indian Official.* In 1851, while Resident at the Court of Lucknow (Oude), and at the request of the Governor General the Marquess of Dalhousie, he wrote *A Journey Through the Kingdom of Oude* in 1849 – 1850 describing the actual conditions of that kingdom, and with the view of pointing out the best measures to be suggested to the King for the improvement and amelioration of the country and people.

The Rajah of Hasunpoor Bundooa mentions, as a fact within his own knowledge, besides the other, for the truth of which he vouches, that in the year 1843, a lad came to the town of Hasunpoor, who had evidently been brought up by the wolves. He seemed to be twelve years of age when he saw him — was very dark, and ate flesh, whether cooked or uncooked.

He had short hair all over his body when he first came, but having, for a time, as the Rajah states, eaten salt with his food, like other human beings, the hair by degrees disappeared. He could walk, like other men, on his legs, but could never be taught to speak. He would utter sounds like wild animals, and could be made to understand signs very well. He used to sit at a bunneea's shop in the bazaar, but was at last recognized by his parents, and taken off. What became of him afterwards he knows not.

The Rajah's statement regarding this lad is confirmed by all the people of the town, but none of them know what became of him.

5. First Sultanpur Wolf Boy

About the year 1843, a shepherd of the village of Ghutkoree, twelve miles west from the cantonments of Sultanpur, saw a boy trotting along upon all fours, by the side of a wolf, one morning, as he was out with his flock. With great difficulty he caught the boy, who ran very fast, and I brought him home. He fed him for some time, and tried to make him speak, and associate with men or boys, but he failed. He continued to be alarmed at the sight of men, but was brought to Colonel Gray, who commanded the first Oude Local Infantry, at Sultanpur. He and Mrs. Gray, and all the officers in cantonment, saw him often, and kept him for several days. But he soon after ran off into the jungle, while the shepherd was asleep. The shepherd, afterwards, went to reside in another village, and I could not ascertain whether he recovered the boy or not.

Major-General Sir W. H. Sleeman

6. The Bankipur Wolf Boy

Zoolfukar Khan, a respectable landholder of Bankipur, in the estate of Hasupur, ten miles from the Sultanpur cantonments, mentions that about eight or nine years ago a trooper came to town, with a lad of about nine or ten years of age whom he had rescued from wolves among the ravines on the road; that he knew not what to do with him, and left him to the common charity of the village, that he ate everything opened to him, including bread, but before taking it he carefully smelt at it, and always preferred undressed meat to everything else; that he walked on his legs like other people when he saw him, though there were evident signs on his knees and elbows of his having gone, very long, on all fours; and when asked to run on all fours he used to do so, and went so fast that no one would overtake him; how long he had been with the trooper, or long it took him to learn to walk on his legs, he knows not. He could not talk, or utter very articulate sounds. He understood signs, and heard exceedingly well, and would assist the cultivators in turning trespassing cattle out of their fields, when told by signs to do so. Boodhoo, a Brahmin cultivator of the village, took care of him, and he remained with him for three months, when he was claimed and taken off by his father, a shepherd, who said that the boy was six years old when the wolf took him at night some four years before; he did not like to leave Boodhoo, the Brahmin, and the father was obliged to drag him away. What became of him afterwards he never heard. The lad had no hair upon his body, nor had any dislike to wear clothes, while he saw him. The statement confirmed by the people of the village.

7. The First Lucknow Wolf Boy

This account of the First Lucknow Wolf Boy is an extract from *A Journey Through the Kingdom of Oude* written by Captain William Sleeman, chief agent to Lord William Bentinck (British governor-general of India, 1833-35) who with the cooperation of the authorities in a number of Indian princely states, succeeded in eliminating the thugs (Hindi Thag, Sanskrit Sthaga ("thief," "rogue"), member of a well-organized confederacy of professional assassins who travelled in gangs throughout India for several hundred years) that from 1831 to 1837 no fewer than 3,266 thugs had been captured, of whom 412 were hanged, 483 gave evidence for the state, and the remainder were transported or imprisoned for life. The fraternity presumably thereafter became extinct.

About seven years ago a trooper belonging to the King and in attendance on Rajah Hurdut Sing of Bondee, alia, Bumnotee, on the left bank on the Ghagra river, in the Bahraetch district, was passing near a small stream which flows into that river, when he saw two wolf cubs and a boy drinking in the stream. He had a man with him on foot, and they managed to seize the boy, who appeared to be about ten years of age. He took him up on the pummel of his saddle, but he was so wild and fierce that he tore the trooper's clothes and bit him severely in several places, though he had tied the hands

together. He brought him to Bondee, where the Rajah had him tied in his artillery gun-shed, and gave him raw flesh to eat; but he several times cut his ropes and ran off; and after three months the Rajah got tired of him, and let him go. He was then taken by a Cashmeeree mimic, or comedian (bhand), who fed and took care of him for six months; but at the end of that time he also got tired of him (for his habits were filthy), and let him go to wander about the Bondee bazaar.

He one day ran off with a joint of meat from a butcher's shop, and soon after upset some things in the shop of a bunneeah, who let fly an arrow at him. The arrow penetrated the boy's thigh. At this time Sanatjllah, a cashmere merchant of Lucknow, was at Bondee, selling some shawl goods to the Rajah, on the occasion of his brother's marriage. He had many servants with him, and among them Janoo, a khidmutgar lad, and an old sipahee, named Ramzan Khan. Janoo took compassion upon the poor boy, extracted the arrow from his thigh, had his wound dressed, and prepared a bed for him under the mango tree, where he himself lodged, but kept him tied to a tent-pin. Janoo, with the consent of his master, gave him rice and pulse to eat. He rejected them for several days, and ate nothing; but Janoo persevered, and by degrees made him eat the balls which he prepared for him; he was fourteen or fifteen days in bringing him to do this.

The odour from his body was very offensive, and Janoo had him rubbed with mustard-seed soaked in water, after the oil had been taken from it (khullee), in the hope of removing this smell. He continued this for some months, and fed him upon rice, pulse, and flour bread, but the odour did not leave him. He had hardened marks upon his knees and elbows, from having gone on all fours. In about six weeks after he had been tied up under the tree, with a good deal of beating and rubbing of his joints with oil, he was made to stand and walk upon his legs like other human beings.

He was never heard to utter more than one articulate sound, and that was "aboodeea," the name of the little daughter of the Cashmeer mimic, who had treated him with kindness, and for whom he had shown some kind of attachment. In about four months he began to understand and obey signs. He was by them made to prepare the hookah, put lighted charcoal upon the tobacco, and bring it to Janoo, or present it to whomsoever he pointed out.

One night while the boy was lying under the tree, near Janoo, Janoo saw two wolves come up stealthily, and smell at the boy. They then touched him, and he got up; and instead of being frightened, the boy put his hands upon their heads, and they began to play with him. They capered around him, and he threw straw and leaves at them. Janoo tried to drive them off but he could not, and became much alarmed; and he called out to the sentry over the guns, Meer Akbur Allee, and told him that the wolves were going to eat the boy. He replied, become away and leave him, or they will eat you also; but when he saw them begin to play together, his fears subsided and he kept quiet. Gaining confidence by degrees, he drove them away; but, after going a little distance, they returned, and began to play again with the boy. At last he succeeded in driving them off altogether. The night after three wolves came, and the boy and they played together. A few nights after four wolves came, but at no time did more than four come. They came four or five times, and Janoo had no longer any fear of them; and he thinks that the first two that came must have been the two cubs with which the boy was first found, and they were prevented from seizing him by recognizing the smell. They licked his face with their tongues as he put his hands on their heads.

Soon after his master, Sanaollah, returned to Lucknow, and threatened Janoo to turn him out of his service unless he let go the boy. He persisted in taking the boy with him, and his master relented. He had a string tied to his arm, and led him along by it, and put a bundle of clothes on his head. As they passed a jungle the boy would throw down the bundle and try to run into the jungle, but on being beaten, he would put up his hands in supplication, take up the bundle and go on; but he seemed soon to forget the beating, and did the same thing at almost every jungle they came through. By degrees he became quite docile. Janoo was one day, about three months after their return to Lucknow, sent away by his master for a day or two on some business, and before his return the boy had ran off, and he could never find him again. About two months after the boy had gone, a woman, of the weaver caste, came with a letter from a relation of the Rajah, Hurdut Sing, to Sanaollah, stating that she resided in the village of Chureyakotra, on his estate, and had had her son, then about four years of age taken from her, about five or six years before, by a wolf; and, from the description which she gave of him, he, the Rajah's relation, thought he must be the boy whom his servant, Janoo, took away with him. She said that her boy had two marks upon him, one on the chest of a boil, and one of something else on the forehead; and as these marks corresponded precisely with those found upon the boy, neither she nor they had any doubt that he was her lost son. She remained for four months with the merchant Sanaollah, and Janoo, his kidmutghur, at Lucknow; but the boy could not be found, and she returned home, praying that information might be sent to her should he be discovered. Sanaollah, Janoo, and Ramzan Khan, are still at Lucknow, and before me have all three declared all the circumstances here stated to be strictly true.

The boy was altogether about five months with Sanaollah and his servants, from the time they got him; and he had been taken about four months and a half before. The wolf must have had several litters of whelps during the six or seven years that the boy was with her. Janoo further adds, that he, after a month or two, ventured to try a waist-band upon the boy, but he often tore it off in distress or anger. After he had become reconciled to this, in about two months, he ventured to put upon him a vest and a pair of trousers. He had great difficulty in making him keep them on, with threats and occasional beatings. He would disencumber himself of them whenever left alone, but put them on again in alarm when discovered; and to the last often injured or destroyed them by rubbing them against trees or posts, like a beast, when any part of his body itched. This habit he could never break him of.

Rajah Hurdut Sewae, who is now in Lucknow on business, tells me (28th January, 1851) that the sowar brought the boy to Bondee, and there kept him for a short time, as long as he remained; but as soon as he went off, the boy came to him, and he kept him for three months; that he appeared to him to be twelve years of age; that he ate raw meat as long as he remained with him, with evident pleasure, whenever it was covered to him, but would not touch the bread and other dressed food put before him; that he went on all fours, but would stand and go awkwardly on two legs when threatened or made to do so; that he seemed to understand signs, but could not understand or utter a word; that he seldom attempted to bite anyone, nor did he tear the clothes that he put upon him; that Sanaollah, the Cashmeeree merchant, used at that time to come to him often with shawls for sale, and must have taken the boy away with him, but he does not recollect having given the boy to him. He says that he never himself sent any letter to Sanaollah with the mother of the boy, but his brother or some other relation of his may have written one for her.

8. The LoboWolf Girl of Devil's River

In 1835, a group of American colonists, led by Dr. Charles Beale, were camped at Lake Espantosa, a renowned haunted location near what is now Carrizo Springs in southwest Texas. Half a mile away from the Beale group, John Dent and his pregnant wife Mollie Pertul Dent, both from Georgia, had built a brush cabin. Dent had come to trap beaver in the Devil's River area, north of the present day Del-Rio, but was also on the run from the law for the murder of a fellow trapper in Georgia. The Dents were to prove fortunate in their choice of a site distant from the lake. A band of Commanches raided the main Beale camp and massacred most of the inhabitants, afterwards throwing the bodies of the victims and their carts into the lake.

A Haunted Location

Apparently even at this time Espantosa Lake had acquired a reputation throughout this part of Texas for ghostly goings-on, this incident adding to the store of ill-luck and sorrow centering on what, to this day Mexicans consider a haunted location, the name Espantosa meaning 'frightful'. A mysterious ghostly fog, a lake monster and a spectral headless rider are some of the ghosts that have been recorded at this supposedly haunted location.

As Mollie was approaching the end of her pregnancy, the couple were reluctant to travel despite the danger of hostile Indians. One night in May 1835, there was a severe thunderstorm and Mollie went into labour. Without the help of modern medicine or the aid of a nurse or doctor Mollie was having problems with the birth and Dent needed to do something about it so he decided to ride westward for help. He arrived at a Mexican goat ranch on the Pecos Canyon, and told them desperately about his wife's condition, begging for someone to ride back with him.

But as the Mexicans prepared their horses to leave there was a furious crash of thunder and a bolt of lightning struck Dent from his horse killing him instantly. After a considerable delay the goat herders mounted up and followed Dent's directions. However, darkness fell before they had got over the divide to Devil's River, thus delaying the search. Finally, at sunrise the next morning they located the Dent's isolated cabin.

But what they found outside the cabin, in an open brush arbor, was Mollie Dent lying dead, alone. She had apparently died in childbirth, but there was no trace of the baby anywhere. The child was never found, but fang marks on the woman's body and numerous wolf tracks over the area made the goat herders naturally assume that the infant had either been devoured or carried off by lobo wolves.

First Sighting of the Wolf Girl in Texas

But this was just the beginning of the story. Ten years later, in 1845, a boy living at San Felipe Springs (Del-Rio) reportedly saw 'a creature, with long hair covering its features, that looked like a naked girl' attacking a herd of goats in the company of a pack of lobo wolves. The story was ridiculed by many, but still managed to spread back among the settlements. Around a year after this incident, a Mexican woman at San Felipe claimed she had seen two large wolves and an unclothed young girl devouring a freshly killed goat. She approached close to the group, she said, before they saw her and ran off.

The woman noticed that the girl ran initially on all-fours, but then rose up and ran on two feet, keeping close to the wolves. The woman was in no doubt about what she had seen, and the scattering of people in the Devil's River country began to keep a sharp watch for the girl.

More Texas Stories of the Wolf Girl

There were similar reports by others in this region of Texas during the following year and Apache stories told of a child's footprints, sometimes accompanied by hand prints, having been found among wolf tracks in sandy places along the river. A hunt was organised to capture the 'Lobo (or Wolf) Girl of Devil's River' as she had now become known, comprising mainly Mexican vaqueros. On the third day of the hunt the naked girl was sighted near Espantosa Lake running with a pack of wolves.

The cowboys managed to separate the girl from her wolf companions and cornered her in a canyon, where she fought like a wildcat clawing and biting frantically to keep her freedom. They finally managed to lasso her to keep her still, but while they were tying her up she began to make frightening, unearthly sounds somewhere between the scream of a woman and the howl of a wolf. As she howled, the monster he-wolf from whom she'd become separated appeared and rushed at her captors.

Fortunately one of the cowboys reacted quickly and shot it dead with a pistol, at which the wolf girl fell into a faint. Securely bound, the men were now able to examine the girl and noted that despite a body covered in hair and her wild mannerisms, her appearance was human. Her hands and arms were well muscled but not out of proportion, and she lacked the ability to speak, only making deep growling noises. She moved smoothly on all fours, but was rather awkward when made to stand up straight.

The girl was put on a horse and taken to the nearest ranch, an isolated two-roomed shack amid the desert wilderness. She was put in one of the rooms and unbound, the cowboys offering her a covering for her body and food and water, but she refused, cowering in the darkest corner. They then left her alone for the night, locking the door and posting a guard outside. The only other opening in the room was a small boarded up window.

Ghostly Cries

But as night fell the cowboys heard terrifying howls coming from the wolf girl's room. The strange cries carried through the still night air, unsettling her captors and soon finding answers from among the wolf pack in the wilderness beyond the shack. Soon there were long deep howls coming from all sides as the pack drew closer to the house, and occasionally strange howling screams from the girl answering them from inside her dark room.

Suddenly the large pack of wolves charged into the corrals, attacking the goats, cows and horses and bringing the cowboys outside shooting and yelling to drive them away. In all the confusion the wolf girl managed to tear the planks from the window and escape into the night. The howls soon abated and the wolves crept back into the wilderness. The next day not a trace of the girl could be found.

Devil's River Sighting

Though there were a few unverified reports in the following years of a young hair-covered girl being seen with a wolf pack in the area, no one ever came in close contact with her. Meanwhile gold had been discovered in California and westward travel had increased significantly. In 1852 a surveying party of frontiersmen searching for a new route to El Paso were riding down to the Rio Grande at a bend far above the mouth of Devil's River. They were almost at the water's edge when they saw at close range, sitting on a sand bar, a young woman suckling two wolf cubs. Suddenly she saw them, quickly grabbed the pups and dashed into the breaks at such a rate that it was impossible for the horsemen to follow.

The girl would have been seventeen years old that year. After that she disappeared into the wilderness forever. It is impossible now to know what became of Mollie Dent's daughter, presuming that's who the wolf girl was. There were subsequent reports of 'human-faced' wolves in the area right up until the 1930s, and author L.D. Bertillion (see sources below), wrote in 1937, 'during the past forty years I have in the western country met more than one wolf face strongly marked with human characteristics'.

The Ghost of Devil's River

The story of the Wolf Girl of Devil's River reads more like a Texas folktale than a real feral child case, and the large amount of evidence for what happened is all anecdotal. She does, however, seem to live on in a more subtle form; her 'ghost' has apparently been seen in the old San Felipe Springs area beside the banks of Devil's River. In 1974 a hunter in this area claimed to have seen her again, in the form of a white apparition which vanished before his eyes.

Back in the autumn of 1835, when John and Mollie Dent had newly arrived in Texas, Mollie wrote her mother an odd letter. It said merely -

'*Dear Mother,*
The Devil has a river in Texas that is all his own and it is made only for those who are grown.
Yours with love
Mollie'.

9. Second Sultanpur Wolf Boy

In all parts of India, the Hindus have a notion that the family of a man who kills a wolf, or even wounds it, goes to utter ruin; and so also the village within the boundaries of which a wolf has been killed or wounded... Some Rajput families in Oude, where so many children are devoured by wolves, are getting over this prejudice.

There was at Sultanpur a boy who was found alive in a wolf's den, near Chandour, about ten miles from Sultanpur, about some years ago. A trooper sent by the native governor of the district of Chandour, to demand payment of some revenue, was passing along the bank of the river near Chandour about noon, when he saw a large female wolf leave her den, followed by three whelps and a little boy. The boy went on all fours and seemed to be on the best possible terms with the old dam and the three whelps, and the mother seemed to guard all four with equal care. They all went down to the river and drank without perceiving the trooper, upon his horse watching them. As soon as they were about to turn back, the trooper pushed on to cut off and secure the boy; but he ran as fast as the whelps could, and kept up with the old one. The ground was uneven, and the trooper's horse could not overtake them.

They all entered the den, and the trooper assembled some people from Chandour with pick-axes, and dug into the den. When they had dug in about six or eight feet, the old wolf bolted with her three whelps and the boy.

The trooper mounted and pursued, followed by the fleetest young men of the party; and as the ground over which they had to fly was more even, he headed them and turned the whelps and the boy back upon the men on foot, who secured the boy and let the old dam and the three cubs go on their way.

They took the boy to the village but had to tie him for he was very restive, and struggled hard to rush into every hole or den they came near. They tried to make him speak, but could get nothing from him but an angry growl or snarl. He was kept for several days at the village, and a large crowd assembled every day to see him. When a grown-up person came near him, he became alarmed, and tried to steal away; but when a child came near him, he rushed at it, with a fierce snarl like that of a dog, and tried to bite it. When any cooked meat was put before him, he rejected it in disgust; but when any raw meat was offered, he seized it with avidity, put it on the ground under his paws, like a dog, and ate it with evident pleasure. He would not let anyone come near him while he was eating, but made no objection to a dog coming and sharing his food with him. The trooper remained with him four or five days, and then returned to the governor, leaving the boy in charge of the Rajah of Hasunpur. He related all that he had seen, and the boy was soon after sent to the European officer commanding the First Regiment of Oude Local Infantry at Sultanpur, Captain Nicholetts, by order of the Rajah of Hasunpur, who was at Chandour, and saw the boy when the trooper first brought him to that village. This account is taken from the Rajah's own report of what had taken place.

Captain Nicholetts made him over to the charge of his servants, who took great care of him, but could never get him to speak a word. He was very inoffensive except when teased, Captain Nicholetts said, and would then growl surlily at the person who teased him. He had come to eat anything that was thrown to him, but always prefered raw flesh, which he devoured most greedily.

He would drink a whole pitcher of buttermilk when put before him. He could never be induced to keep on any kind of clothing even in the coldest weather. A quilt stuffed with cotton was given to him when it became very cold this season, but he tore it to pieces, and ate a portion of it – cotton and all, with his bread every day. He was very fond of bones, particularly uncooked ones, which he masticated apparently with as much ease as meat. He ate half a lamb at a time without any apparent effort, and was very fond of taking up earth and small stones and eating them. His features were coarse, and his countenance repulsive; and he was very filthy in his habits. He continued to be fond of dogs and jackals, and all other small four-footed animals that came near him; and always allowed them to feed with him if he happened to be eating when they approached.

Captain Nicholetts in letters dated the 14th and 19th of September, 1850, said that the boy died in the latter end of August, and that he was never known to laugh or smile. He understood little of what was said to him, and seemed to take no notice of what was going on around him.

He formed no attachment for anyone, nor did he seem to care for anyone.

He never played with any of the children around him, or seemed anxious to do so. When not hungry he used to sit petting and stroking a pareear or vagrant dog, which he used to permit to feed out of the same dish with him. A short time before his death Captain Nicholetts shot this dog, as he used to eat the greater part of the food given to the boy, who seemed in consequence to be getting thin. The boy did not seem to care in the least for the death of the dog. The parents recognized the boy when he was just found, Captain Nicholetts believes; but when they found him to be so stupid and insensible, they left him to subsist upon charity. They then left Hasunpur, and the age of the boy when carried off cannot be ascertained; but he was to all appearances about nine or ten years of age when found, and he lived about three years afterwards. He used signs when he wanted anything, and very few of them except when hungry, and he then pointed to his mouth. When his food was placed at some distance from him, he would run to it on all fours like any four-footed animal; but at other times he would walk upright occasionally. He shunned human beings of all kinds, and would never willingly remain near one. To cold, heat, and rain he appeared to be indifferent; and he seemed to care for nothing but eating. He was very quiet, and required no kind of restraint after being brought to Captain Nicholetts. He had lived with Captain Nicholetts' servants about two years, and was never heard to speak till within a few minutes of his death, when he put his wolf-children hands to his head and said, "It ached," and asked for water. He drank it and died.

10. The Chupra Wolf Boy

At Chupra, twenty miles east from Sultanpur, lived a cultivator with his wife and son, who was then three years of age. In March, 1843, the man went to cut his crop of wheat and pulse, and the woman took her basket and went with him to glean, leading her son by the arm. The boy had lately recovered from a severe scald on the left knee which he got in the cold weather, from tumbling into the fire, at which he had been warming himself, while his parents were at work. As the father was reaping and the mother gleaning, the boy sat upon the grass. A wolf rushed upon him suddenly from behind a bush, caught him up by the loins, and made off with him towards the ravines. The father was at a distance at the time, but the mother followed, screaming as loud as she could for assistance. The people of the village ran to her aid, but they soon lost sight of the wolf and his prey.

She heard nothing more of her boy for six years, and had in that interval lost her husband. At the end of that time, two *sipahees* came, in the month of February, 1849, from the town of Singramow, which is ten miles from Chupra, on the bank of the Khobae rivulet. While they sat on the border of the jungle, which extended down to the stream, watching for hogs, which commonly come down to drink at that time in the morning, they saw there three wolf cubs and a boy come out from the jungle, and go down together to the stream to drink. The *sipahees* watched them till they had drunk and were about to return, when, they rushed towards them. All four rap towards a den in the ravines.

The *sipahees* followed as fast as they could; but the three cubs had got in before the *sipahees* could come up with them, and the boy was half way in when one of the *sipahees* caught him by the hind leg, and drew him back. He seemed very angry and ferocious, bit at them, and seized in his teeth the barrel of one of their guns, which they put forward to keep him off, and shook it. They however secured him, brought him home, and kept him for twenty days. They could for that time make him eat nothing but raw flesh and they fed him upon hares and birds. They found it difficult to provide him with sufficient food, and took him to the bazaar in the village of Koeleepoor; and there let him go to be fed by the charitable people of the place till he might be recognized and claimed by his parents. One market-day a man from the village of Chupra happened to see him in the bazaar, and on his return mentioned the circumstance to his neighbours. The poor cultivator's widow, on hearing this, asked him to describe the boy more minutely, when she found that the boy had the mark of a scald on the left knee, and three marks of the teeth of an animal on each side of his loins, the widow told him that her boy when taken off had lately recovered from a scald on the left knee, and was seized by the loins when the wolf took him off, and that the boy he had seen must be her lost child.

She went off forthwith to the Koelee bazaar, and in addition to the two marks above described, discovered a third mark on his thigh, with which her child was born. She took him home to her village, where he was recognized by all her neighbours. She kept him for two months, and all the sporting landholders in the neighbourhood sent her game for him to feed upon. He continued to dip his face in the water to drink; but he sucked in the water, and did not lap it up like a dog or wolf. His body continued to smell offensively. When the mother went to her work, the boy always ran into the jungle, and she could never get him to speak. He followed his mother for what he could get to eat, but showed no particular affection for her; and she could never bring herself to feel much for him; and after two months, finding him of no use to her, and despairing of ever making anything of him, she left him to the common charity of the village. He soon after learned to eat bread when it was given to him, and ate whatever else he could get during the day, but always went off to the jungle at night. He used to mutter something, but could never be got to articulate any words distinctly. The front of his knees and elbows had become hardened from going on all fours with the wolves. If any clothes are put on him he takes them off, and commonly tears them to pieces in doing so.

He prefered raw flesh to cooked, and would feed on carrion whenever he could get it. The boys of the village were in the habit of amusing themselves by catching frogs and throwing them to him; and he would catch and eat them. When a bullock would die, and the skin removed he would go and eat it like a village dog. The description was given of him by the mother herself, who was still living in Chupra at the time. She had never experienced any return of affection for him, nor had he shown any such feeling for her. Her story was confirmed by all her neighbours, and by the head landholders, cultivators, and shopkeepers of the village.

11. The Shajehanpur Wolf Boy

This appeared in Lippincott's Magazine, LXI, 189 8, p121:

Also Mr. Greig, late of the 93 rd (Sutherland) Highlanders declares that when his regiment was marching toward Bareilly in 1858, after the taking of Lucknow, he saw at Shahjehenpur an individual said to have been, as a child, taken away from his village by wolves, brought up by them, and to have lived with them for several years. He appeared to be about twenty years of age; his body was covered with short brown hair; his powers of speech extended to nothing beyond low grunts, and he could not be induced to wear any kind of clothing. Whenever he saw raw meat he rushed for it and devoured it greedily. The story was that he had been ridden down and caught by a native after a long chase, and that he did not run on his feet like a human being, but on all fours like an animal.

This letter from H D Willock of the Bengal Civil Service appeared in The Field, 11 Jan 1896, no 2246 pp 36-7:

You ask me if I ever heard of a wolf boy mentioned by an officer of the 93rd Highlanders as having been seen by him at the Rosa Sugar Factory (situated some three mites from Shahjehanpur) in 1858. I saw such a boy, or rather a man, and had opportunities of learning his history and observing his condition and habits. I have every reason for supposing that the man alluded to by the officer spoken of was the same I also saw. I was posted to Shahjehanpur in September, 1858, shortly after the re-occupation of the district, and, going into camp at once, returned to the station in the following month. It was then that I heard of the presence of a "wolf boy" in the city. I found him occupying a hut in a serai allotted to him by the proprietor. He was to all appearance about twenty years of age, in manners and habits a mere animal. He was dumb, but able to show signs of pleasure or anger by sounds which may be described as grunts. He wore no clothing, save a rag which had to be tied around his waist. He could stand, but invariably crawled, the skin of his knees being hardened like leather. He occupied his hut at night only, passing the day in prowling about the city, receiving and eating scraps of food thrown to him by the residents, who regarded him as one afflicted by the Deity, and as such a fit object for charity. At night he lay in his hut curled up on a bed of straw, which supplied all his requirements; while a blanket placed for his use by me was disregarded and unused. He formed no attachments, and seemed to be devoid of passions or intellect.

I remained at Shahjehanpur till 1865, and saw him frequently. He was, I believe, alive when I left. In 1857 all public offices were destroyed, and I was unable to find any file or record giving particulars of his early life. But from a reappointed member of the magistrate's staff, I heard that some fourteen years previously, a mounted orderly, when returning from the magistrate's camp in the forest, saw a wolf cross his path, followed by a figure which he at once recognised as that of a boy. It ran at no great pace on its hands and knees. He dismounted and captured it after a short chase. It bit and scratched with great energy, but he took it to Shahjehanpur. It naturally attracted great attention, but all attempts made to reclaim it from its acquired habits failed, and eventually it had to be abandoned to the only life suitable to it, which it was leading when I saw it. I was living when first at Shahjehanpur with G. P. Money, the magistrate, and R. R. Carew, manager of Rosa Factory. They have passed away, and I cannot think of anyone to whom I can refer you for further particulars of the case. I may say that full credence to the wolf boy story was given by Messrs. Money and Carew. The latter had resided at Rosa for many years previous to the Mutiny, and the story was not new to him.

12. The Third Sultanpur Wolf Boy

This description of the Third Sultanpur Wolf Boy is taken from a letter written to The Field, London, no 9, 1895, no 2237 p 786.

When I was Assistant-commissioner of Sultanpur, Oude, shortly after the Mutiny had been quelled, either in 1860 or 1861, the police brought in a male child which they declared they had recovered from a wolf den. Whether this was true or not I cannot positively assert, but inquiries were made at the time, and there seemed no reason for doubting it.

As regards the child, I saw him when he was just brought in, and almost daily until I left the station. He seemed to be about four years old, and sat up like a dog, both arms straight down in front of him, with his hands flattened out on the ground, and his legs drawn up under him like a dog; he moved by hops something like a monkey, but never stood up on his legs, and always kept his hands on the ground. He gave vent to snarls and sounds, not actual barks like a dog, but something between a bark and a grunt. He would not touch cooked food, but ate raw meat ravenously. The police officer took charge of him, and gradually broke him in to taking milk, then milk and bread, and so on. He certainly was not an idiot, for, after being tamed, he was sent to school, and eventually taken into the police force. Everyone at the time considered it a clear case of a wolf-child. Whether such things are, or were, will always be a disputed point. I see no reason against it, and the natives thoroughly believe in the idea: but at the same time, they believe in many legends which are absolutely absurd.

13. Dina Sanichar

Sources include Valentine Ball's Jungle Life in India, and numerous letters, reports and newspaper articles. Much of this material, along with details of almost every recorded pre-1940 case, is in Wolf-Children and Feral Man by Singh and Zingg.

Found in a Wolves' Cave

Dina Sanichar, one of the boys who lived at the Sekandra orphanage, is usually assumed to have been mentally sub-normal. He was removed from a wolves' cave in 1867 when he was about six years old.

Captured by Hunters

Dina Sanichar was discovered when hunters in the jungles of Bulandshahr were astonished to see a boy follow a wolf into her den, running on all fours. They smoked out the wolf and her companion and (as usual) shot the wolf.

Dina Sanichar's Feral Characteristics

Like so many other feral children, he initially exhibited all the habits of a wild animal, tearing off clothes and eating food from the ground. He was eventually weaned off raw meat onto cooked, but never did learn to speak. He apparently became addicted to tobacco. Dina Sanichar died in 1895.

14. The Second Sekandra Wolf Boy

That Sekandra Orphanage Again

The second Sekandra wolf boy is the second wolf boy we know of to be cared for at the Sekandra orphanage. He was smoked out of a wolf's den in 1872, and exhibited the usual characteristics of only liking raw meat, crawling around on all fours, and a lack of speech. Unfortunately, he died after only four months at the orphanage.

Sikandra approach

The Second Sekandra Wolf Boy Meets Dina Sanichar

The second Sekandra wolf boy arrived at the orphanage while Dina Sanichar was still there; not surprisingly, Dina befriended the younger boy, and taught him to drink out of a cup.

15. The Batsipur Wolf Boy

An account of the Batsipur wolf boy taken from the Indian Mirror (of Calcutta) on Sunday, the 19th February 1893:

"Babu Bhagelu Singh, a Zemindar of the Bhagalpore District, lately came out for hunting in his diara lands near a village called Bazitpore, a few miles off Dalsingsarai Station, on the Tirhut and Bengal Northwestern Railway. As he was aiming at a wild animal, he found someone like a human being at a distance entering the jungle, as if through fear. This aroused his curiosity, and he ordered his followers to hunt for the object.

After a diligent search they found a boy, about fourteen years old, who was stark naked. He has been brought from the jungle and kept in the Cutcharry-barry of the Zemindar Babu at Bazitpore. He cannot speak, but can laugh and make a chattering sound. He does not eat any cooked things, etc., but eats everything raw, such as raw fish, frogs, etc. When catching frogs or such other living creatures, he walks on all fours, and jumps on his

Dalsingsarai Station present day

prey like a cat. If the prey is secured, he at once puts it in his mouth and devours it. Daily a large number of people resort to the place to have a look at him. If money or any other metallic things are given to him, he throws them away. He is now being taught to eat cooked food, and has learnt to eat fried rice. Still he wears no clothes, and never enters a place of shelter save that of a tree. Lately he was attacked with cholera, and the Zemindar Babu having attempted to administer some medicines, he fled from his Cutcharry to a river bank, and there drank water to his heart's content, and thus escaped out of the clutches of the fell disease. In all respects he resembles a man, the only difference is that he cannot speak. It is not known how he got into the jungle. Some say that either he was lost during his infancy, or thrown away by his parents owing to their extreme poverty, while others say that he was carried away from his cradle by a wild animal where he grew up under providential care. But the popular belief is that he is a Yogi. In case any of your readers be inclined to satisfy his curiosity, he may find the boy at village Bazitpore, near the Dalsingsarai Railway Station on the Tirhut and Bengal Northwestern Railway."

16. The Satna Wolf Boy

Hutton's Child

All we know about the Satna Wolf Boy is what Professor J H Hutton reported in his address to the Folk Lore society, which he later published as Wolf-Children in Folk-Lore, 1940, vol 51, pp 9-13 (and for that reason, he's sometimes referred to as "Hutton's Child").

Carried off by Wolves

Apparently, this boy was seen in 1916 at Satna, Rewa State, India, by a Mr C. H. Burnett, who was told that the boy had been carried off by wolves as a baby, and rescued years afterwards. He couldn't speak and "had very peculiar habits".

17. The Wolf Girls of Midnapore – Kamala and Amala

In 1920, however, a case came to light that was too well documented to be dismissed so simply. In that year, Reverend Joseph Singh, a missionary in charge of an orphanage in Northern India, heard of two ghostly spirit figures seen accompanying a band of wolves near Midnapore in the Bengal jungle. The local villagers were fearful of these apparitions but local custom forbid them to do any harm to the wolves. Intrigued, Singh built a hide in a tree top over-looking the lair of the wolf pack, an old ten-foot high termite mound that had become hollowed out with time. As the moon rose, Singh saw the wolves come out one by one. Then sticking their heads out briefly to sniff the night air before bounding forwards into the clearing came two hunched and horrible figures. As Singh described the "ghosts" in his diary, they were: "Hideous looking...hand, foot and body like a human being; but the head was a big ball of something covering the shoulders and the upper portion of the bust…Their eyes were bright and piercing, unlike human eyes…Both of them ran on all fours."

Singh returned some days later with a large hunting party to dig the creatures out. In his journal, he says that as the first pick-axe blows landed on the termite mound, the she-wolf came rushing out, baring her fangs and barring the way. She had to be shot dead with a volley of arrows. The

hunting party then broke into the lair and hauled out the two human children, along with two wolf cubs. The children turned out to be two girls, aged about three and five. Their ghastly appearance came from the mass of matted hair on their heads and their hunched four legged gait. Otherwise they appeared lithe and healthy. Surprisingly, the two appeared not to be sisters but girls taken at separate times – further evidence of some distorted maternal instinct in the mother wolf. When no-one in the local villages came forward to claim the girls, Singh took them back to his orphanage, christening the elder one, Kamala, and the younger, Amala.

Singh knew nothing of the stories of other feral children such as Victor and the Hessian wolf-boys, but his description of Kamala and Amala were strikingly similar. The girls seemed to have no trace of humanness in the way they acted and thought. It was as if they had the minds of wolves. They tore off any clothes put on them and would only eat raw meat. They slept curled up together in a tight ball and growled and twitched in their sleep. They only came awake after the moon rose and howled to be let free again. They had spent so long on all fours that their tendons and joints had shortened to the point where it was impossible for them to straighten their legs and even attempt to walk upright. They never smiled or showed any interest in human company. The only emotion that crossed their faces was fear. Even their senses had become wolf-like. Singh claimed their eyes were supernaturally sharp at night and would glow in the dark like a cat's. They could smell a lump of meat right across the orphanage's three acre yard. Their hearing was also sharp – except, like Victor, the voice of humans seemed strangely inaudible to their ears.

A poor but relatively well educated man, Singh did his best to rehabilitate his charges. Influenced by the horticultural model of child development, he theorised that the wolf habits acquired by Kamala and Amala had somehow blocked the free expression of their innate human characteristics. Singh felt it was his job (not least, for religious reasons) to wean the girls from their lupine ways and so allow their buried humanity to emerge. Unhappily, before his experiment had progressed far, the younger girl, Amala, sickened and died. This proved a great set-back to Kamala, who had only just started to lose her fear of other humans and her orphanage surroundings. Kamala went into a prolonged mourning and for a while, Singh feared for her life as well. But eventually Kamala recovered and Singh started a patient programme of rehabilitation.

First, Singh had to socialise Kamala. Through a combination of massage to loosen the limbs and the dangling of food just out of reach, Singh coaxed Kamala into standing and walking. She never learnt to walk smoothly and would often revert to all fours, especially if she wanted to run, however Singh saw this as literally the first step towards getting her to "shake off" her wolf-like habits. Gradually, Singh trained Kamala to accept other human ways, teaching her to eat normal food, to sleep with the other children and to welcome the company of fellow humans.

Singh was relatively successful in changing Kamala's outward behaviour, getting her walking and housetrained within a couple of years of her capture. But when it came to teaching her to speak, Singh struggled. Just before she died, Amala had been making promising progress towards speech, giving voice to the babbling and cooing noises that mark the first stage in a normal child's learning to talk. With Kamala, progress was much slower but Singh persevered. After three years, Kamala had mastered a small vocabulary of about a dozen words. After several more years, her vocabulary had increased to about 40. To compare, a normal two-year-old child, at the peak of its language learning, would find it easy to pick up 40 new words in a single week. Also, Kamala's words were only partly-formed and her grammar stilted. The Hindi word for medicine is ashad but Kamala would only pronounce half the word, saying "ud".

Likewise, she would say bha for bhat (rice), bil for biral (cat) and tha for thala (plate).

Singh made much of an incident when Kamala was given some dolls to play with and then a box to keep them in. Kamala shut the dolls away and "proudly" told the other children in the orphanage: "Bak-poo-voo." Singh interpreted this utterance as standing for "Baksa-pootool-vootara," — Hindi for "Box-doll-inside." While this broken sentence marks a significant step forward for a girl who was little more than a wolf cub a few years earlier — showing not just a use of language but the first glimmerings of a social awareness – Kamala's speech still fell a long way short of normally-reared children.

The story of Singh and his two wolf-girls broke in the newspapers in 1926. As one London paper noted: "At clubs frequented by big game hunters and explorers it was the chief topic at the lunch table." In fact arguments became so heated about whether the story could be true or not that the next day, the same paper was reporting on a fist fight breaking out between two members of just such a gentleman's club over the story. However, the wolf-girls did not become a topic of debate within the scientific community until two books were published over a decade later, one by Arnold Gesell, the noted Yale University child specialist, and one by Robert Zingg, a Denver anthropologist, both of which were based on the diary kept by the Reverend Singh.

Gesell summed up Kamala's progress, saying that at the age of 16, after nine years in the care of the orphanage, she still had the mind of a three and a half year old. But slow though Kamala's progress was, Gesell felt her story demonstrated just how mentally naked humans are when born and how much we rely on society to shape us. As he put it, human culture operates on the mind as "a large scale moulding matrix, a gigantic conditioning apparatus" without which we would remain at the level of animals. However, while more open-minded than most about the importance of a social mould in forging man's higher mental abilities, Gesell still was wedded to a horticultural view of mental development. He believed that culture "unlocks" our dormant abilities rather than, as the bifold model suggests, that these abilities are grafted on top of the raw material of the animal mind. So, for example, Gesell saw the gradual appearance of smiles and other sociable expressions on Kamala's face as the result of the loosening of rigid muscles rather than thinking that Kamala might have had to learn such emotional signals through contact with her fellow humans. Like Singh, Gesell spoke of Kamala's wolf-like habits as if they were just an overlay of copied behaviours that thinly papered over her true human nature — or as he put it: "motor sets [which] constituted the core of her action-system and affected the organisation of her personality."

Gesell wondered whether, with a few more years, Kamala would have caught up eventually with other normal children or whether the traumas of her early years had left her somehow permanently stunted. The question was never answered because in 1929, Kamala caught typhoid and died. Her last words to Singh's wife — possibly too poignant to be true — were said to have been: "Mama, the little one hurts."

18. The Jhansi Wolf Boy

Rescued From a Wolves' Cave

The Jhansi wolf boy was "rescued" from the cave where he lived with wolves. Estimates of his age varied between 7 and 12. As might be expected, he walked on all fours, couldn't speak, and lapped water. Oddly, however, he ate grass, and appeared to have subsisted on roots and other plants, rather than raw meat. (This suggests an isolated existence, rather than living with wolves.)

19. Ramu, the Second Lucknow Wolf Boy

Ramu, the Second Lucknow Wolf Boy

Ramu was found in 1954 — possibly in a third-class waiting room at Lucknow station — and taken to the Balrampur hospital on 17 January, and was aged around 10-12.

Ramu's Feral Credentials

Like many feral children, Ramu had calloused knees and hands, and is reported to have also had pointed teeth and scars on the back of his neck. He couldn't speak but made animal noises instead. Ramu also only liked raw fruits and meat when first taken to Balrampur, but after only a few weeks had taken to cooked vegetables and bread.

Reunited with his parents

The following report is from *The Hindu*, dated 10 February 1954:

> The seven-year-old 'Wolf Boy', who has been an inmate at the local Balrampur Hospital since January 17, has found his parents. It is claimed they belong to the Khatick community and live in Lucknow. According to them, Ramu, as this child is known, was snatched away by a wolf when asleep from the lap of his mother one night six years ago. Frantic efforts were made to trace him, and finally he was believed to have died. A chance

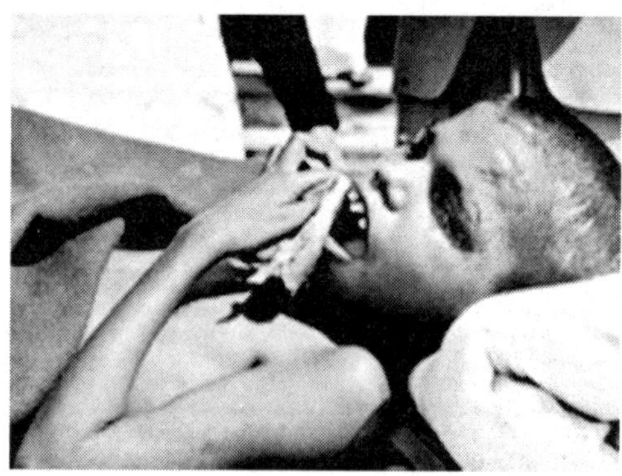

visit to Balrampur Hospital following press reports led to the recognition of the 'Wolf Boy' by his parents, who identified him by a mark over his forehead and a bluish patch on his right thigh.

Ramu's Affinity with Wolves

Ramu was not interested in the company of other humans and particularly feared adults, but when taken on an outing to the zoo became very excited by the wolves. This, together with the fact that Ramu lapped milk from a glass, tore his food apart and was happy to chew on bones for hours, suggested to doctors that he had been brought up by wolves.

What Became of Ramu?

Ramu spent the next 14 years at Lucknow hospital and newspapers report that he died there on 20 April 1968.

20. Djuma, the Wolf Boy from Turkmenistan

Djuma was found in 1962 in southern Russia by oil explorers, and exhibited the usual characteristics of feral children: he howled like a wolf and savagely bit one of the oilmen.

Djuma Ate Raw Meat

The name Djuma means the Wolf Boy. Still alive in 1991 (when he would have been about 37) Djuma was unable to walk; he ate raw meat, and would bite people when frightened, although he could brush his teeth and hair and use the lavatory. Djuma had learnt a very limited amount of language, amounting to only a few ungrammatical phrases.

A Victim of Civil Unrest

Djuma has apparently communicated to his carers using sign language that his family were killed in a political purge, his mother throwing herself over his body to save him.

If alive today, he is presumably still in the clinic where he was expected to live out his days, spending much of his time in a world of his own, oblivious to his surroundings.

21. Pascal, Shamdeo, a Sultanpur Wolf Boy

Shamdeo Found with Wolves

Shamdeo was originally rescued from the forest of Musafirkhana, about 32km from Sultanpur, by Narsing Bahadur Singh, the headman of the village of Narangpur. He had discovered the boy playing with four or five wolf-cubs in May of 1972.

Feral Characteristics

On discovery, Shamdeo (called Shamdev by Chatwin, and later re-named Pascal and also Baloo), had very dark skin, fingernails grown into claws, a tangle of matted hair and callouses on his palms, elbows and knees. Although he ran quickly on all fours, he couldn't escape Singh who captured him and took him home.

Shamdeo hated the sun and sought out dark corners: he became restless after dark. Like Kamala and others, he caught chickens

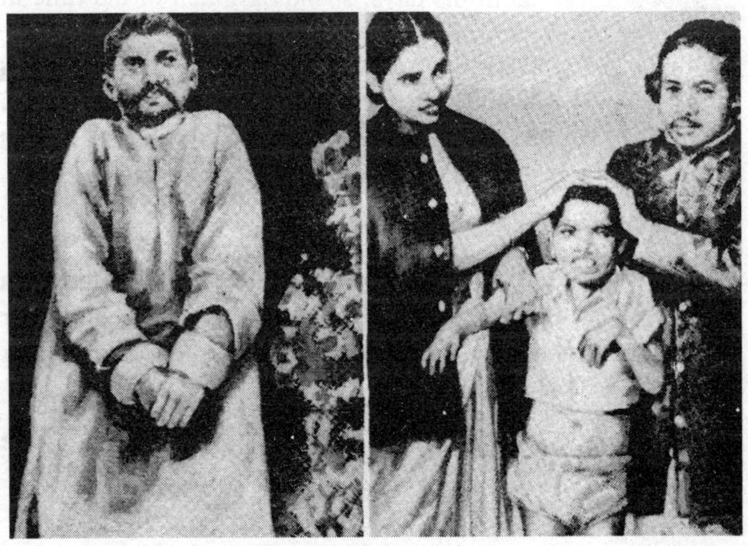

alive and ate the whole bird, including the entrails; he was also strongly attracted to the smell of blood.

Shamdeo's Escape

He lived with Singh for some five months, but presumably escaped, as he was subsequently sighted roaming around scavenging for scraps.

The sisters of Mother Teresa's Mission of Charity found him at a house whose owner said a laundrywoman (presumably, his mother) had come to claim him but declined to take him back, so he was taken by the sisters into their orphanage. During his first week there, Shamdeo would rip off his clothes and throw his food away, plate and all, and only gradually settled into orphanage life.

Visited by Bruce Chatwin

Shamdeo was visited at the Mission by Bruce Chatwin who tells the story in *What Am I Doing Here?*; Chatwin then went on to meet Singh, who took Chatwin with him to reclaim "his" boy from the Mission. By this time, Shamdeo had taken to using one or two simple signs to communicate, and the callouses had gone.

Shamdeo recognised Singh immediately and jumped to greet him. However, chastened by the Sisters' firmness, Singh forgot his plans to reclaim the child but instead asked if he might visit again.

True or Hoax?

Chatwin remained convinced that Singh had spoken the truth about having found the boy in the company of wolf-cubs, after having witnessed Singh's grilling at the hands of a former barrister.

Children Raised by the Leopards and Jackals

1. The Leopard Boy of Dihungi

Stolen From the Fields

Like so many feral children, the leopard boy of Dihungi was stolen while his mother worked in the fields — in this case, she was cutting rice near her village of Dihungi. The villagers had found and killed two leopard cubs two days previously, and the mother had been haunting the outskirts of the village.

Found Three Years Later

Three years later, a sportsman killed a leopardess close to the village, and reported that there were still cubs alive. The villagers eventually captured two cubs and the boy, who was identified by and returned to his parents.

Leopard-Like Speed

When found, the Leopard boy of Dihungi was able to run at speed on all fours, but when Stuart Baker saw him some five years later he was managing to walk. He had an acute sense of smell, and when first returned to the village would seize any fowl within his reach, tear it to pieces, and eat it.

Source

Stuart Baker writing in *The Journal of the Bombay Natural History Society*, vol 27, July 1920, pp 117-118 visited the Leopard boy of Dihungi, and his report is reproduced in *Wolf-Children and Feral Man* by Singh and Zingg.

2. The Indian Jackal Girl

This girl (of European origin) was apparently rescued from a pack of jackals and then kept for a time by the Maharini of Cooch Bahar. Like so many other "rescued" children, she longed to return to the jungle, and died within a few months.

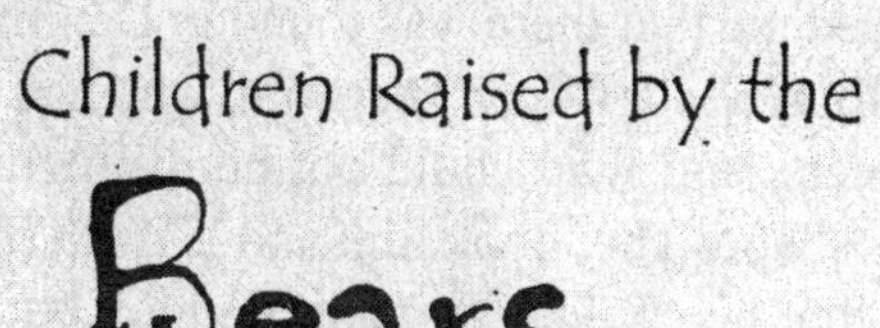

Children Raised by the Bears

1. The Danish Bear Boy

The Danish Bear Boy is yet another boy about which there is scant information. Lucilio Vaninin, garrotted by the Inquisition in 1619, had, in a pre-evolutionary discussion of the origin of the human race, made the following footnote (translated by Bendysche in The Anthropological Treatises of Johann Friedrich Blumenbach):

A man of credit assured me that there was found in Denmark, a young man of about fourteen or fifteen years old, who had lived in the woods with bears, and who could not be distinguished from them but by his shape. They took him and learned him to speak; he said then, that he could remember nothing but only since the time they took him from amongst the bears.

2. Joseph, the First Lithuanian Bear Boy

How Many Boys?

As in the case of the boys of Hesse, we have many confusing reports about these boys, giving different dates and quantities of Lithuanian bear-boys. After a review of the various sources, it looks like we are dealing with probably only two incidents (totalling three boys).

Joseph, the First Lithuanian Bear-Boy

The first Lithuanian bear-boy (Joseph) dates from 1657, 1661, 1663 or 1669, depending who you believe. For details of some of the sources, see Wolf Children and Feral Man, by Singh and Zingg.

Caught by Hunters

Joseph was one of two boys seen in the woods by hunters. Although they caught Joseph, the other boy escaped. Joseph was about 9 years old, and was taken before the King of Poland in Warsaw. He disliked wearing clothes, but did learn to walk upright and eat cooked meat; however, he never learned to speak well. He and the other boy had possibly been left behind inadvertently when their families fled from raiding Tartars.

3. The Second Lithuanian Bear-Boy

The second Lithuanian bear-boy, caught in 1694, did acquire some speech and was taught to walk upright. More information is provided in this extract from Condillac's Essai sur l'Origine des Connaissances Humaines:

> It is certainly believed all over the kingdom, that children have been frequently nurtured by bears, who are very numerous in these woods [of Lithuania].
>
> There was one kept in a convent in my time who was taken among them, as I have described in my Latin Treatise [Evangel. Medici, Art 15, p. 181] of the Suspensions of the Laws of Nature. He was about ten years of age (which might be guessed only by his stature and aspect) of a hideous countenance, and had neither the use of reason nor speech: he went about on all four, and had nothing in him like a man, except his human structure: but seeing he resembled a rational creature, he was admitted to the font, and christened; yet still he was restless and uneasy, and often inclined to fright. But at length, being taught to stand upright, by clapping up his body against a wall, and holding after the manner that dogs are taught to beg; and being by little and little accustomed to eat at table, he after some time became indifferently tame, and began to express his mind with a hoarse and unhuman tone; but being asked concerning his course of life in the woods, he could not give much better account of it, than we can do of our actions in the cradle.
>
> Sir, I shall endeavour to satisfy your request and to give you an account of a boy that I saw at Warsaw in the year 1669, who had been brought up by bears. Coming to this city of Poland with design to be present at the election of a king after John Casimir, who had abdicated the crown, I enquired

what was worth seeing in or about this place: whereupon I was informed, among other things, that there was in the suburbs of this city (which go towards King Casimir's palace) in a nunnery, a certain male child, who had been brought up among bears and who had been taken some time before at a bear-hunting.

Upon this information I went immediately to that place to satisfy my curiosity, where I found the aforesaid boy, playing under the pent-house before the nunnery gate. His age, as well as I remember, I guessed to be about twelve or thirteen. As soon as I came near him he leaped towards me as if surprised and pleased with my habit. First, he caught one of my silver buttons in his hand with a great deal of eagerness, which he held up to his nose to smell; afterwards he leaped all of a sudden into a corner, where he made a strange sort of noise not unlike a howling. I went into the house, where a maidservant informed me more particularly of the manner of his being taken. But having not with me the book wherein I wrote my observations in my travels, I cannot possibly give you an exact account of it. This maid servant called the boy in, and showed him a good large piece of bread; which when he saw, he immediately leaped upon a bench that was joined to the wall of the room, where he walked about on all-four: after which, he raised himself upright with a great spring, and took the bread in his two hands, put it up to his nose, and afterwards leaped off from the bench upon the ground, making the same odd sort of noise as before. I was told that he was not yet brought to speak, but that he hoped in a short time he would, having his hearing good. He had some scars on his face, which were commonly thought to be scratches of the bears.

Thus, Sir, you have all that I can remember of a curiosity, which I saw so long time since; the truth of which nobody ought to question, since there are several parallel examples in history.

Sir,

Your most affectionate servant,

J P Van den Brande de Cleverskerk.

For another confirmation of this matter of fact, I have the testimony of an authentic author, M. Christopher Hartnoch of Passenheim in ducal Prussia, who writ two books of the state of Poland. He says that during the reign of King John Casimir, in the year 1669, there happened an accident which perhaps might hardly be credited by posterity; which was that there were then two boys found by a company of soldiers among the bears in the woods near Grodna; one of which, as soon as he saw the bears assaulted, fled into the neighbouring morass, while the other endeavouring likewise to escape, was taken by the soldiers and brought to Warsaw, where he was afterwards christened by the name of Joseph.

He was about twelve or thirteen years old, as might be guessed by his height, but his manners were altogether bestial; for he not only fed upon raw flesh, wild honey, crab-apples and such like dainties which bears are used to feat with, but also went, like them, upon all-four. After his baptism he was not taught to go upright without a great deal of difficult, and there was less hope of ever making him learn the Polish language, for he always continued to express his mind in a kind of bear-like tone. Some time after King Casimir made a present of him to Peter Adam Opalinski, Vice Chamberlain of Posnan, by whom he was employed in the offices of his kitchen, as to carry wood, waters etc., but yet could he never be brought to relinquish his native wildness, which he retained to his dying-day; for he would often go into the woods amongst the bears, and freely keep company with them without any fear, or harm done him, being, as was supposed, constantly acknowledged for their fosterling.

4. The Bear Girl of Fraumark

Found in a Cave

In 1767 the inhabitants of Fraumark in lower Hungary, pursuing a bear in the mountains, came to a cave in which a completely naked wild girl was found. She was tall, robust, and seemed to be about eighteen years old. Her skin was brown and she looked frightened.

Ate Raw Meat

Her behaviour was very crude. Although they had to use violence to make her leave the cave, like many other feral children the Bear Girl of Fraumark didn't cry or shed any tears. Finally they succeeded in bringing her to Karpfen, a small town in the county of Atlsohl, where she was locked up in an asylum. In common with other feral children, she would only eat raw meat.

Place Names

Like many places in Europe, Karpfen has changed its name many times and has moved between various countries on numerous occasions in history. It is currently known as Krupina, Slovakia.

5. The Jalpaiguri Bear Girl

The following story is from *Amrita Bazar Patrika* of 14 December 1892. It is a little unusual in that the child learnt to laugh.

One of the missionaries of the New Dispensation Church (the late Babu Keshub Sen's Brahmo Somaj), in his recent tour of Jalpaiguri, came across an idiot girl of about eight years of age. The girl roved through the streets, appeasing her appetite with whatever food the people offered her, and at night slept under trees or under the open sky. The history of the girl is wonderful. We sometimes read in books of legendary stories of human beings nursed by lions, wolves, and bears, the girl is a living instance of such nursing. The girl has the features of the hill people. She was discovered by some coolies belonging to a tea garden in the den of a bear. It is presumed that she was brought there by some unaccountable circumstances, and when very young was nursed by her bear-mother.

When just taken out of the den, she was a strange combination of a bear and a man, she was ferocious like a bear, and attempted to bite and scratch men when she saw them. In her locomotion she used her legs as well as her hands and moved like a bear. She growled at intervals like a bear and ate and drank as a bear; in short, all her habits were like those of a bear, while by her features no one could fail to recognize her as a human being. The police afterwards took her under their custody; this happened when she was about three years of age. She was then put in the Jalpaiguri hospital, where she forgot much of her strange habits.

She learnt to walk, eat, and drink like a human being, and showed certain emotions which were peculiar to man. The hospital authorities retained her about three years, and afterwards thinking her an incurable discharged her. The said missionary, who is the manager of an orphanage, took pity on her, and brought her down to the office of the Unity and the Minister newspaper (organ of the New Dispensation Church of the late Babu Chunder Sen) at No. 20, Patuatolla Lane, Calcutta. When we first saw her we were greatly impressed by her amiable and innocent appearance. She is rather bulky and has long hair. Even now she has not forsaken bear-like growls, and it is with some difficulty that she can walk like man. The only emotion which she incessantly expresses is by means of smiles, which oftentimes develop into loud laughter. She is more a laughing girl than anything else. She does not seem to understand human language, though her powers of hearing and seeing have been found on examination to be unimpaired. When food was brought to her, she readily stretched forth her hand to grasp it, and when she was in possession of it, or when she was engaged in consuming it, she laughed loudly and her smiles and laughter at times appeared very attractive and sweet. If there is anything about her that commands human sympathy, it is her smile, The Orphanage being considered an unsuitable place for her, she has been removed to the Das Asram, a philanthropic institution of Calcutta, founded by some Brahmo gentlemen on the lines of the Salvation Army, to afford an asylum to the poor and homeless waifs and strays of the Calcutta streets, where she is now taken care of. Hundreds of men and women now go to see her daily but she shows an aversion to being exhibited as an object of curiosity before a large number of people. By contact with society she is now generally acquiring human habits. It has been pronounced by medical men that she will gradually regain her humanity.

6. Goongi

Caught Aged 14

Goongi was caught in July of 1914 when she was about 14 years old. She was given the name Goongi, and because that means dumb we can infer that she wasn't able to speak. Goongi was found in the jungle near Naini Tal, in the Indian state of Uttarakhand. She exhibited characteristics common to feral children: she was supposedly covered with hair, and ran on all fours.

Brought Up by Bears?

Our information comes from Jim Corbett (Jim Corbett's India) and he suggests that she had been brought up by bears, owing to the similarity of her dietary habits to that of bears — she wouldn't eat cooked food — and her climbing agility. She also had deep scratches that could have been caused by bears.

7. The Turkish Bear Girl

Captured by Hunters

One Ali Osman, hunting on Mt Olympus with his companion Bahri, killed an enormous she-bear and was then attacked by what he described as a howling wood-spirit that made his hair stand on end. Eventually he succeeded in overpowering the creature and realised she was just a little girl. They tied her up with their belts, and found, he said, conclusive proof in the bear's lair that a human being had lived there.

Where Did the Turkish Bear Girl come From?

Enquiries by Maranz at the village of Mussalilar revealed that 8 years previously, a woman (Fatma) with a three-month-old child who had arrived at the village looking for work left her daughter on the ground while gathering brushwood in the forest. A she-bear carried off the daughter, and Fatma left the village soon after, unable to bear the sight of Mt Olympus.

The Turkish bear girl was taken to the hospital for the mentally ill at Bakirkey.

Children Raised by the Apes

1. The Monkey Boy of Casamance

Of the Child of Casamance we know very little. A naked tanned boy aged around 16 arrived in a village one evening. He climbed like the monkeys he is said to have been raised by. Although he was not deaf — he was taught to obey commands — the Child of Casamance couldn't speak.

2. Assicia, the Liberian Monkey Girl

Assicia Emerges From the Forest

Some time before 1940, Assicia appeared from the virgin forest in Liberia, and is assumed to have been brought up by chimpanzees. Assicia moved around on all fours, on knees and fingertips, with ankles bent, scratched herself in the manner of a monkey, and uttered quivering cries.

Assicia (Sylvana) Never Spoke

Assicia was renamed Sylvana (presumably because of her forest origins), never learnt to speak, and her favourite food was bananas.

Source

Assicia receives extensive coverage in Le Livre des Enfants Sauvages by André Demaison.

3. Tissa, the Monkey Boy of Sri Lanka

Found with Monkeys

Tissa was found in Sri Lanka in 1973, when seen walking on all fours with a group of monkeys near the village of Tissamaharama. Tissa was discovered by a woman wood-cutter called Pemawathie who captured him and named him Tissa, but handed him to the police because of his wild ways.

Tissa's Feral Credentials

As well as walking on all fours, Tissa exhibited other animal characteristics such as yelping and snarling at humans and eating his food off the ground, and in common with most feral children did not smile.

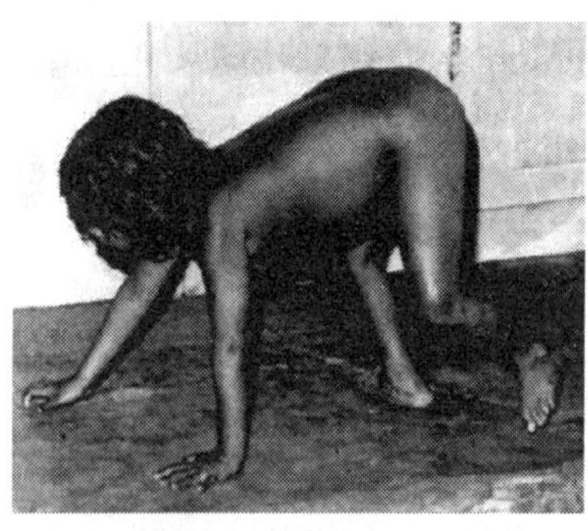

Tissa Makes Progress

However, after three months in a welfare home near the Sri Lankan capital Colombo, Tissa could smile and take food to his mouth with his hand, but couldn't talk and was still learning to stand and walk without assistance. The home, run by a Miss L. P. Morawake, had apparently cared for two other animal boys in the past.

4. Baby Hospital, the Monkey Girl from Sierra Leone

This seven year old girl found by an Italian missionary in Sierra Leone, and given the unlikely name of Baby Hospital. She was seemingly brought up by apes or monkeys. Baby Hospital was unable to stand upright and crawled instead of walking, and ate directly from her bowl without using her hands. She made the chattering noises of apes or monkeys.

Baby Hospital's arms and hands were reported to be well developed, but not her leg muscles. She resisted attempts to civilise her, instead spending much of her time in an activity that is very unusual for feral children: crying.

5. Robert, a Monkey Boy from Uganda

Robert, a Victim of Civil War

Robert lost his parents in the Ugandan civil war at the age of three in 1982, when Obote's looting and murdering soldiers raided their village, around 50 miles from Kampala. Robert then lived in the wild, presumably with Vervet monkeys, for three years until he was found by soldiers in 1985. One adult female monkey attempted to protect Robert from his captors.

Unable to Speak

During his three years in the wild, Robert will have survived on a diet of fruit and berries. When found, he couldn't sit or stand, but only squat, and would never smile. After two years in a Kampala orphanage, Robert was toilet trained but still couldn't talk.

6. Saturday Mthiyane (Saturday Mifune)

An Authentic Feral Child

Saturday Mthiyane (or Mifune) is our most credible story of a child who lived with animals. A living primary source, a direct witness, saw the boy of around 5 in the company of monkeys over a period of a year, in the Kwazulu-Natal province of South Africa.

Saturday Mthiyane

Saturday visited human habitations along with his troop of monkeys in order to steal food, which is how he came to be noticed and observed. When eventually captured, he was taken to the Ethel Mthiyane school for the disabled, and named Saturday Mthiyane — Saturday because that's the day he was caught, and Mthiyane after the school's head and founder.

Saturday's Feral Characteristics

Saturday exhibited characteristics in common with many other feral children. "He was very violent during his first days here. He used to break things in the kitchen, get in and out through windows. He didn't play with other kids and instead he used to beat them. He liked uncooked red meat," said Ethel Mthiyane. "He didn't like blankets. He wanted to sleep naked and he hated clothing."

Ten Years Later

Saturday is one of the few modern children to have been followed up. When the Johannesburg Mail and Guardian visited the school ten years later, they found that Saturday was still unable to speak. He had been taught to walk, but was still refusing to eat cooked food, preferring raw vegetables instead; bananas remained his favourite fruit.

7. John Ssebunya, the Ugandan Monkey Boy

Domestic Strife

John Ssebunya was born in the mid 1980s, but ran away from home (probably aged around four) after seeing his mother murdered by his own father (who, according to some reports, subsequently hanged himself).

Lived with Monkeys

It is generally accepted that John Ssebunya was cared for at least to some extent by green African (vervet) monkeys while in the jungle.

Captured by Hunters

Details are confused, but it seems John was found by a tribeswoman or girl (called Millie) in 1991, hiding in a tree. She returned with menfolk from the village and, as is so often the case, not only did John resist capture but also his adoptive family came to his defence, throwing sticks at the villagers.

Hypertrichosis

Initial reports suggest John Ssebunya's entire body was covered with hair. When he defecated, he excreted worms over half a metre long.

John Ssebunya Identified

Once captured and cleaned up — he was covered in scars and wounds, with knees scarred from crawling — he was identified as John Ssebunya. He was given by Millie to the care of Paul and Molly Wasswa, who run a charitable foundation for orphans. He couldn't talk or cry initially, but has subsequently learned to speak. This suggests that he may have learned some speech before his stay in the wild.

From Monkey Boy to Choir Boy

John now not only talks but also sings, and tours with the Pearl of Africa children's choir. John was the subject of the BBC documentary Living Proof, screened on 13 October 1999.

8. Bello, the Nigerian Chimp Boy

Abandoned by His Parents

Bello, the Nigerian Chimp Boy was found in 1996, at the age of about two. Both mentally and physically disabled, he had probably been abandoned by his parents at the age of about six months, a common practice with disabled children among the Fulani, a nomadic people who range great distances over the West African Sahel region.

Raised by Chimpanzees?

Believed to have been adopted and raised by chimpanzees, Bello was found with a chimpanzee family in the Falgore forest, 150 km south of Kano in northern Nigeria. When the story reached the news agencies some six years later in 2002, Bello had been living at the Tudun Maliki Torrey home in Kano.

Bello Exhibits Feral Characteristics

When first discovered, Bello walked like a chimpanzee, using his legs but dragging his arms on the ground. He would leap about at night in the dormitory, disturbing the other children, smashing and throwing things. Six years later Bello was much calmer, but would still leap around in a chimpanzee-like fashion, make chimpanzee-like noises, and clap his cupped hands over his head repeatedly.

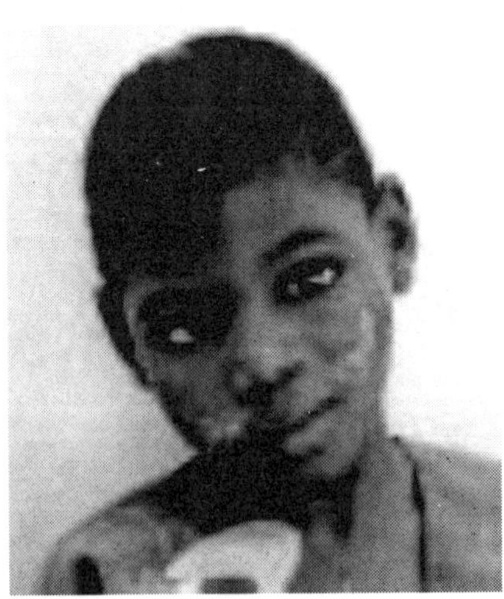

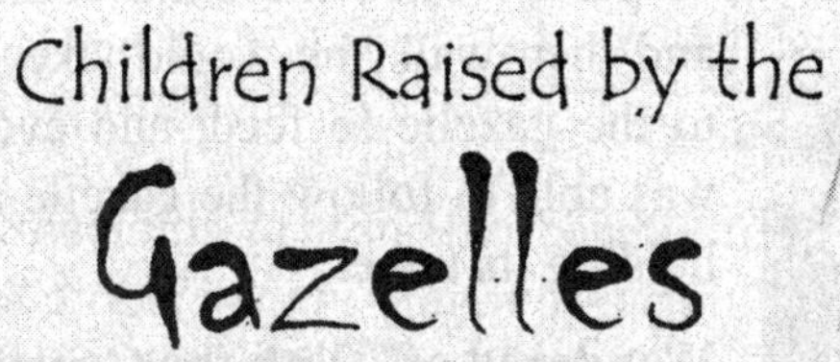

Children Raised by the Gazelles

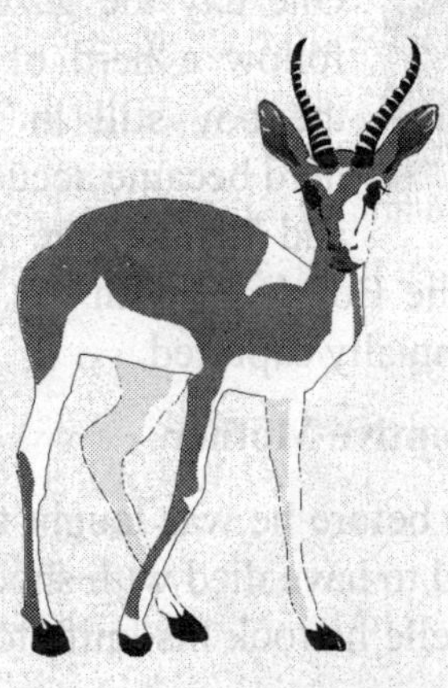

1. The Mauritanian Gazelle Boy

Source

The first gazelle-boy story is from around 1900 and comes from one Sidi Dah Ould Haiba of Dakar.

Wet-nursed by a Gazelle

The boy of Aftout-es-Saheli in former French Mauritania was apparently wet-nursed by a gazelle because his mother was unable to feed him (to use a sheep or goat for such a purpose was not unusual in those parts). Once the child could crawl and then walk, he would take himself to the gazelle to feed, and eventually was able to follow the gazelle around, holding its tether.

Wandered off With the Gazelles

One day the gazelle wandered off to follow a herd of wild gazelles, with the boy still in tow. Eventually the herd became accustomed to the gazelle and her strange companion, and the Mauritanian Gazelle Boy lived with the herd for some years before he was eventually captured.

Kills his Own Adoptive Mother

It was a long time before he was taught to speak. He became a hunter and is said to have died with shock and grief when he realised that a gazelle he took his knife to was his former wet nurse.

2. The Saharan Gazelle Boy

Jean-Claude Auger and the Saharan Gazelle Boy

Jean-Claude Auger, an anthropologist from the Basque country, was travelling alone across the Spanish Sahara (Rio de Oro) in 1960 when he met some Nemadi nomads, who told him about a wild child a day's journey away. The next day, he followed the nomads' directions. On the horizon he saw a naked child "galloping in gigantic bounds among a long cavalcade of white gazelles".

Auger found a small oasis of thorn bushes and date palms and waited for the herd. Three days later, his patience was rewarded, but it took several more days of sitting and playing his galoubet (Berber flute) to win the animals' confidence. Eventually, the child approached him, showing "his lively, dark, almond-shaped eyes and a pleasant, open expression... he appears to be about 10 years old; his ankles are disproportionately thick and obviously powerful, his muscles firm and shivering; a scar, where a piece of flesh must have been torn from the arm, and some deep gashes mingled with light scratches (thorn bushes or marks of old struggles) form a strange tattoo."

The boy walked on all fours, but occasionally assumed an upright gait, suggesting to Auger that he was abandoned or lost at about seven or eight months, having already learnt to stand. He habitually twitched his muscles, scalp, nose and ears, much like the rest of the herd, in response to the slightest noise. Even in deepest sleep he seemed constantly alert, raising his head at unusual noises, however faint, and sniffing around him like the gazelles.

Auger describes how he gradually learnt to decipher the significance of every gazelle gesture and movement, which the boy shared with the herd. There was a complex code of stamping to indicate distance of food sources; and social interaction through exchanges of licking and sniffing, with the boy emitting a kind of mute cry from the back of his throat with his mouth closed. He had one word: kal (khah), meaning stone or rock. One senior female seemed to act as his adoptive mother. He would eat desert roots with his teeth, pucking his nostrils like the gazelles. He appeared to be herbivorous apart from the occasional agama lizard or worm when plant life was lacking. His teeth edges were level like those of a herbivorous animal.

Two years after his stay with the herd, Auger returned with a Spanish army captain and his aid-de-camp, who kept their distance to avoid frightening the herd off. Curiosity eventually overcame them and they chased the boy in a jeep to see how fast he could run. This frightened him off altogether, though he reached a speed of 32-34 mph (52-54 km/h), with continuous leaps of about 13ft (4m). Olympic sprinters can reach only 25 mph (40 km/h) in short bursts.

His pursuers failed to keep up across the rough terrain, and eventually the herd disappeared as the jeep sustained a puncture. In 1966 an unsuccessful attempt was made to catch the boy in a net suspended from a helicopter; unlike most of the feral children of whom we have records, the gazelle boy was never removed from his wild companions. Auger took no photographs of the boy, being more concerned with protecting him from human interference than providing evidence to convince the sceptics of his existence.

The Other Source

According to the fortean zoologist Ivan Sanderson, the story of an earlier gazelle-boy "turned out to be a plant by a bored newsman in Cairo during World War II"; but he gives no further details. The reported version is from Baghdad in August 1946 by a certain M Abdul Karim, and the story bears re-telling. A wild boy had been caught in the desert straddling Transjordan, Syria and Iraq. Amir Lawrence al Sha'alan, chief of the Ruweili tribe, was out hunting in this inhospitable region, whose only inhabitants were the staff at the British-run stations of the Iraq Petroleum Company.

"I was astonished to see what looked like a boy running amid a herd of gazelles we were chasing," said the Amir. "I called to the occupants of the other cars to stop shooting. We were still far away, but could see that the boy was running as fast as the gazelles. We chased the herd in our cars for 50 miles (80km), during which time he kept up with them, bounding along with a half-human, half-animal gait. Suddenly we saw the boy stumble and fall. When we came up to him we found that his leg had been injured by a large stone. He looked up at us with fear starting from his luminous eyes and shrank from our touch, emitting cries like a wounded gazelle."

The Amir tried to feed and clothe him, but he kept escaping, so he took him to Dr Musa Jalbout at one of the Petroleum Company stations, who later passed him into the care of four Baghdad doctors. Dr Jalbout said he acted, ate and cried like any gazelle, and had no doubt that he had lived all his life among the gazelles, being suckled by them and cropping the sparse desert herbage along with the herd. He was thought to be aged about 15.

Apparently speechless, he was covered in fine hair and ate only grass – although a week before Karim's report he had had his first meal of bread and meat. He could allegedly run at 50 mph (80km/h), twice the Olympic record. He was 5ft 6in (1.7m) tall, "so thin that the bones could be counted easily beneath the flesh, yet stronger physically than a normal full-grown man." An unnamed "Syrian expert of desert lore in Damascus" is quoted as saying that Bedouin women giving birth in the desert often abandon their babies to the mercy of nature. Most died, but in very rare cases the child was adopted by animals.

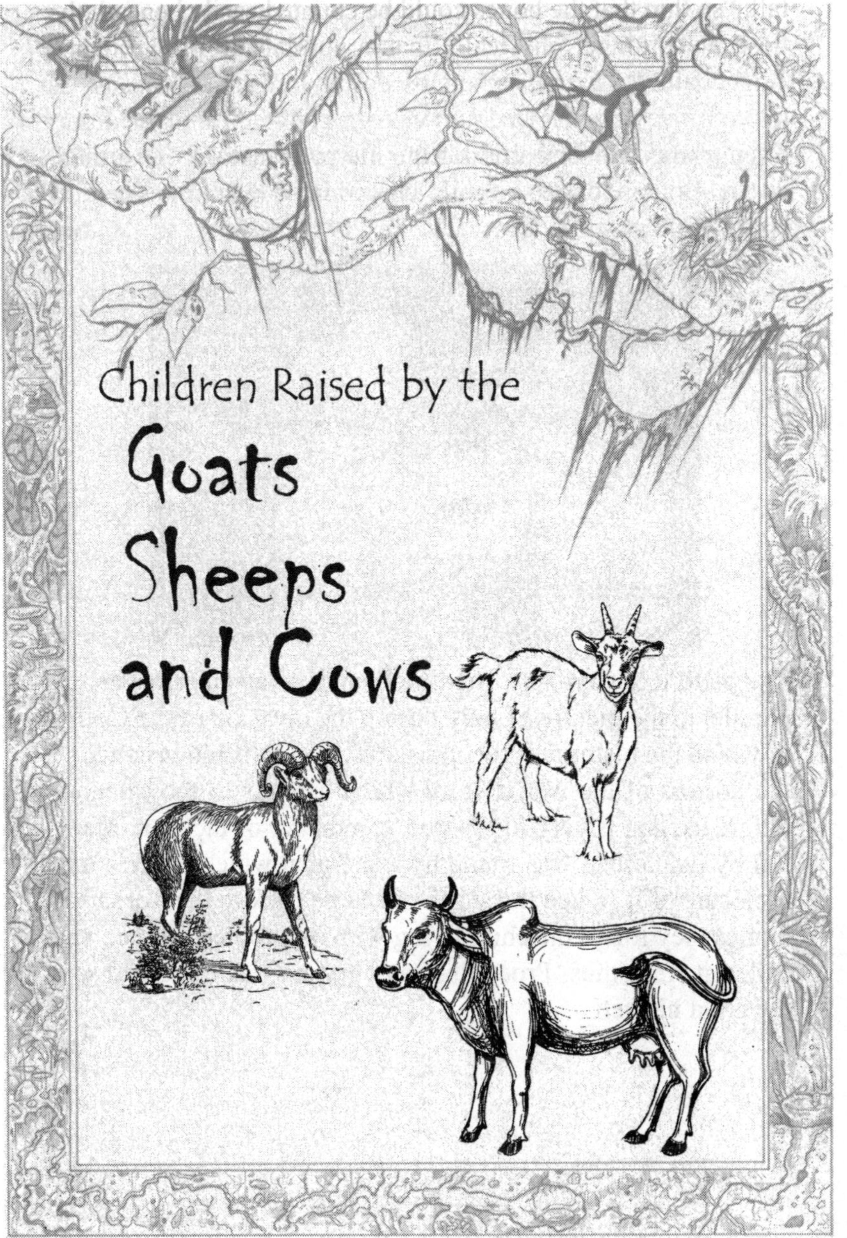

Children Raised by the Goats Sheeps and Cows

1. Aegisthus

Aegisthus, the feral child from Roman times, is described in De Bello Gothico, bk II, ch XVII, quoted by Tylor in Anthropological Review.

The picture of Germany after the French invasion forms an apt parallel to the picture of Italy during the invasion of the Goths, in which the historian Procopius tells, as a startling instance of the horrors of the war, a story which belongs to the category before us, and is very likely true as a matter of fact. An infant, left by its mother, was found by a she-goat which suckled and took care of it. When the survivors came back to their deserted homes they found the child living with its adopted mother, and called it Aegisthus. Procopius says that he was there and saw the child himself.

2. Irish Sheep-Boy

We have very little information about the Irish Sheep Boy. What there is comes from Nicolaes Tulp (Observationes Medicae) where he tells us that this boy resisted capture for some time (sounds familiar), and once caught and returned to human society he exhibited at least three tell-tale signs of the feral child: not wanting to change his diet (from grass and hay), enduring temperature extremes, and not wanting to stay among humans.

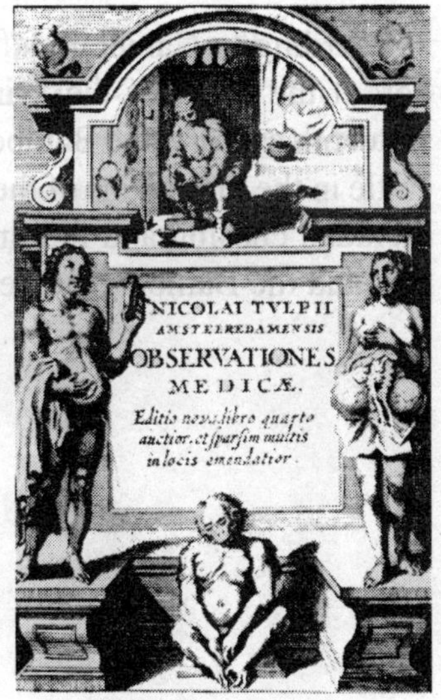

LUGDUNI BATAVORUM
apud GEORGIUM WISHOFF.
M.DCC.XXXVIII

Did the Irish Sheep Boy Live with Sheep?

Tulp says this boy lived among wild sheep, although there is no evidence that there were any wild sheep in Ireland at that time. He was taken to Amsterdam when aged about 16, but Tulp isn't clear about what age he was captured.

3. The Bamberg Boy

According to Camerarius, who says he often used to see this boy at the court of the Prince of Bamberg at the end of the sixteenth century, the Bamberg boy said that he grew up among cattle in the mountains of the region. His wild behaviour, which included chasing and fighting dogs on all fours, gradually left him and the Bamberg Boy eventually even married.

4. Skiron, the Sheep Boy of Trikkala

A Romanian man (from Wallachen) who had settled in Kastania died leaving a wife and several children without means of support. The woman left the youngest child, Skiron, in the care of someone else and returned to her homeland.

The Sheep Boy of Trikkala Escapes

However, the boy escaped from his adopted father and ran wild in the woods for four years, living on milk from the sheep in the summer, and acorns and roots in winter.

Skiron Finds a Home

Skiron was taken into the care of a shepherd, who clothed and fed him.

5. Daniel, the Andes Goat Boy

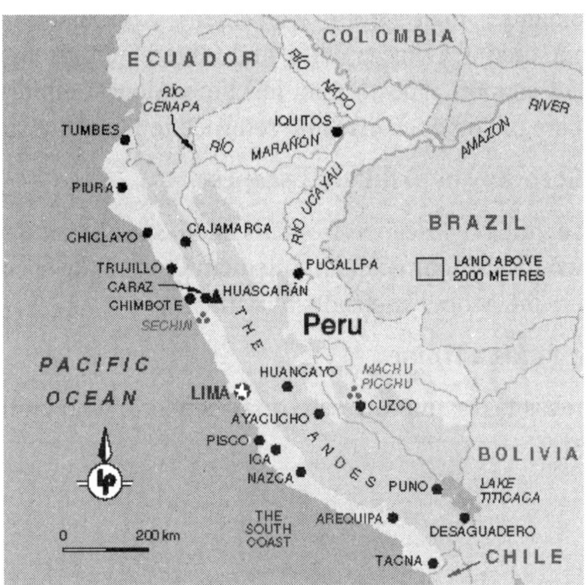

Daniel, the Andes Goat-Boy was found in the Andes, Peru, in 1990, and was said to have been raised by goats for eight years. He is supposed to have survived by drinking their milk, and eating roots and berries. After being found, the Andes Goat-Boy was investigated by a team from Kansas University.

Children Raised by the Dogs

1. Kunu Masela

Kunu Masela is one of those street children who hung around with dogs, in the Kenyan town of Machakos. Once his story received publicity in the local papers, his mother revealed herself, and admitted that poverty had caused her to abandon Kunu at the age of about three. Mrs Rukia Ali Murefu, age 29, was a coffee plantation worker who had moved to Nairobi.

Breast Fed by Dogs

Kunu Masela claims to have been breast-fed by the dog he lived with, which he called Poppy.

2. Ivan Mishukov, the Russian Dog Boy

In 1998, the collapse of the Russian economy meant that some 2 million homeless children in Russia were pretty much left to fend for themselves. One six-year-old boy, Ivan Mishukov, made the headlines in the summer of that year because of his preference for living in the streets under the protection of a pack of wild dogs.

Abandoned by his Parents

Ivan Mishukov chose the streets for his home after he was abandoned by his parents (or, possibly, decided to leave the apartment where his mother lived with her alcoholic boyfriend) at the age of four.

Lived with Dogs

Ivan Mishukov earned the trust of a pack of wild dogs by offering them scraps from the food he managed to beg, and in return for the food, they provided him with protection from the winter temperatures on the streets of Reutova, west of Moscow, which can reach 30 below zero (Celsius).

Caught by Police

Ivan became known to the police, but they could not separate him from the dogs, in spite of three attempts. Each time, the dogs came to the defence of the boy, who by now had lived two years on the streets. Eventually the police managed to separate the pack from Ivan by laying bait for the animals inside a restaurant kitchen. Deprived of his guard dogs, the savagely snarling boy was quickly trapped.

Back to Normality

Because he could talk before his sojourn on the streets, Ivan Mishukov could of course still talk on his return to human society. He spent a short while in the Reutov children's shelter and then started school.

3. Axel Rivas, the Chilean Dog Boy

The Chilean Dog-Boy

Axel Rivas had been thrown out of his home by abusive parents when he was five years old, and was then placed in a children's home. He didn't like it, and escaped in 1998, at the age of eight.

After that Axel lived with a pack of around 15 strays in the Chilean port of Talcahuano, sleeping with them in a cave on the outskirts of the town.

When he was first sighted by police on 16 June 2001, Axel Rivas made an escape attempt by jumping into the Pacific Ocean. He was eventually caught and taken to a children's unit in Conceptión. "The dogs are my family," he told police. "Please let me go back to them."

Feral Characteristics

"He's showing signs of depression, is aggressive and is not speaking much although he does know how to speak," Delia Delgatto, head of Chile's National Child-care Service said of Axel Rivas. "He was dressed almost in rags, was dirty and had filthy hair." His case caused a nationwide scandal in Chile.

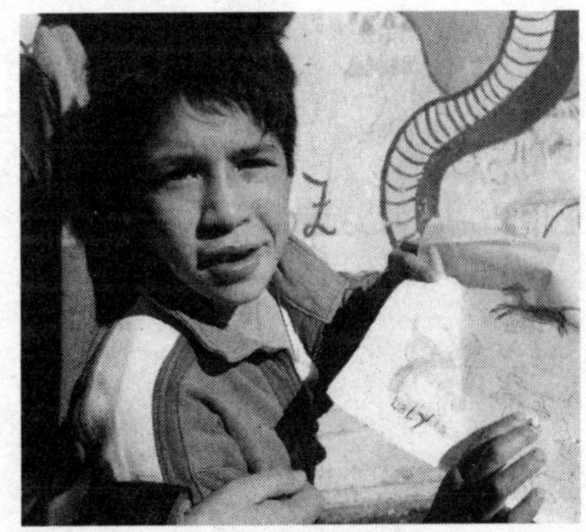

Axel told police that he had sucked the milk of a pregnant dog for sustenance. "Yes, because I was hungry. It was my breakfast," he said. "He lived in a cave with dogs and roamed the streets for food with them. He would eat out of garbage cans and find leftovers," said Delgatto. "He wasn't reared by the dogs as such, he lived with them in a cave," she said.

Axel Rivas Escapes Again

At the beginning of November he ran away again from the children's home where he was being looked after. "He was responding well to psychiatric treatment and his relations with other people were improving but last week he got up and left," spokeswoman Miriam Olate said. Axel is believed to have climbed over a wall to freedom.

Childcare workers said they had been talking to potential foster families before Axel escaped. "We were preparing him for a family atmosphere. His self control and attention were improving." Olate said.

4. Traian Caldarar, the Romanian Dog Boy

Romanian Dog-Boy

Traian Caldarar is a Romanian boy who apparently lived wild, separated from his family, for three years. He is believed to have left the family home because of domestic violence. His mother, Lina Caldarar, said that she loved her son but had a violent partner, who was always beating her. When she lost Traian, she was distraught, and hoped he had perhaps been adopted by another family. She said: "When I fled, I lost contact with Traian, although I tried to get him back. He [the boy's father] didn't allow me to take my child, even though I tried to. He said the child belonged to him."

Traian Caldarar's Developmental Condition

Although aged seven when he was found, Traian Caldarar was only the size of a three year old, could not speak, and was naked and living in a cardboard box covered with a polythene sheet. He suffered from severe rickets, had infected injuries and his circulation was poor, possibly because of frostbite.

Living with Dogs?

Doctors believe it would have been impossible for Traian to survive on his own and speculated that he received assistance from the many stray dogs in the Transylvanian countryside. He was found near the body of a dog that he had apparently been eating.

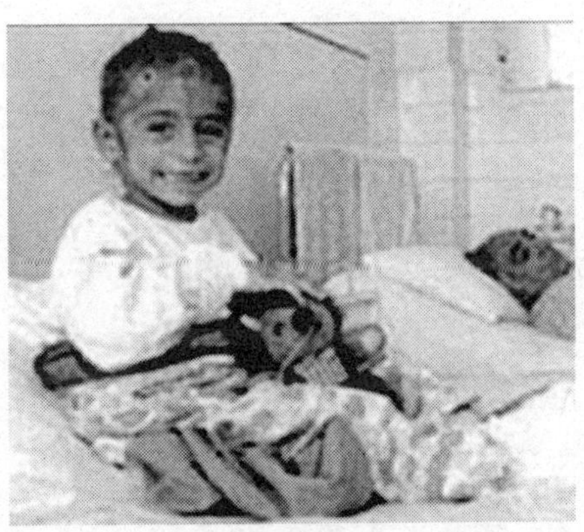

Found by a Shepherd

Traian Caldarar was found after the car of a shepherd, Manolescu Ioan, broke down. Mr Ioan had to walk from his pastures and came across a child who he reported to police, who later captured the boy.

Train Caldarar's Wild Ways

Traian walked with the bandy gait of a chimpanzee and tried to sleep under his bed rather than on it. Dr Mircea Florea said: "He was found in an animal position and his movements are animalistic. The facts show that he was not brought up in a social environment. He becomes very agitated when he does not have food. He is looking for something to eat all the time. He sleeps after he eats."

5. Andrei Tolstyk, the Russian Dog Boy

Andrei Tolstyk appears to be yet another boy who was abandoned by both parents and left to fend for himself and was brought up by the family dog.

First Andrei's mother left when he was just three months old, and then his father abandoned him too.

When finally tracked down by social workers at the age of seven, Andrei exhibited dog-like characteristics.

Full Story of Andrei Tolstyk

The full story (Abandoned boy said to have been raised by a dog) was reported by the New Zealand News dated 04.08.2004 by Andrew Osborn.

"A Mowgli-like wild boy who appears to have been raised by a dog since he was three months old has been discovered living in a remote part of Siberia seven years after he was abandoned by his parents.

Andrei Tolstyk was discovered three weeks ago by social workers who wondered why the seven-year-old had not enrolled at his local school in the beautiful Siberian region of Altai.

Deprived of human contact for so long, Andrei could not talk and had adopted many dog-like traits, including walking on all fours, biting people, sniffing his food before he ate it and general feral behaviour.

In an extraordinary case of life imitating art, Andrei, like Rudyard Kipling's fictional Mowgli in '*The Jungle Book*', had spent almost his entire youth in the company of animals.

According to the local press, his existence had been forgotten.

His mother left home when he was three months old, entrusting Andrei's care to his alcoholic invalid father who also appears to have abandoned the boy soon afterwards and drifted away.

Incredibly, the hamlet of Bespalovskoya where the family lived was so sparsely populated and the house so remote that the parents' absence went unnoticed by the lonely outpost's few other inhabitants.

Instead, Andrei reportedly forged a close bond with the only other living thing around, the family guard dog, which somehow helped the young baby survive and grow up.

Doctors say that Andrei was born with speech and hearing problems anyway but that his wayward parents made no effort with him for the short time that they hung around.

Dubbed a 'dog boy' by some in the Russian media, he has now been moved to a shelter for orphans in a local town where he is being encouraged to mix with other children.

When he first arrived, the shelter staff told RIA-Novosti that he was afraid of people, behaved aggressively and erratically and continued to sniff all his food before eating it. They were, however, able to communicate using basic sign language.

Two weeks after his arrival they say he began to walk on two legs and has since mastered the art of eating with a spoon, making his own bed and playing with a ball.

The other orphans are reported to be suspicious of the boy they call 'wild' but Andrei is said to have struck up a friendship with a little girl with whom he communicates using sign language.

Doctors, paediatricians and psychologists are currently carrying out a series of tests on Andrei to ascertain whether he can be taught normal human behaviour.

If the answer is yes he will be transferred to a normal children's home; otherwise he will be dispatched to a specialised boarding school.

Police have initiated a search for his parents, who are likely to face various charges of neglect and endangerment if and when they are found.

Andrei Tolstyk's is not the first case of 'a feral child' in Russia. In 1998 police near Moscow 'rescued' Ivan Mishukov, then six years old, from the clutches of a pack of wild dogs he had lived with for the last two years.

Mishukov left the family home when he was four to get away from his mother and her abusive alcoholic boyfriend. He took to begging and won the dogs' trust by offering them scraps of food. In return they protected him, from the cold and from ill-wishers, and made him their pack leader. The police tried to rescue him three times but each time he was protected by the dogs.
They eventually managed to separate the boy from the dogs by leaving bait for the pack in a restaurant kitchen.

Mishukov, who could speak before he went wild, has been successfully reintegrated into society though is said to still dream of dogs."

Children Raised by the Birds

1. Sidi Mohamed, the Ostrich Boy

Lived with Ostriches

Sidi Mohamed is another child who never lost his name. He was playing outside at the age of 5 or 6, and wandered off into the bush where he met ostriches who became his foster family.

Caught by Hunters

Some 10 years later Sidi Mohamed was finally caught by men out hunting. During his decade-long ostrich vacation he is said to have lived on grass.

Mysterious Wild Children

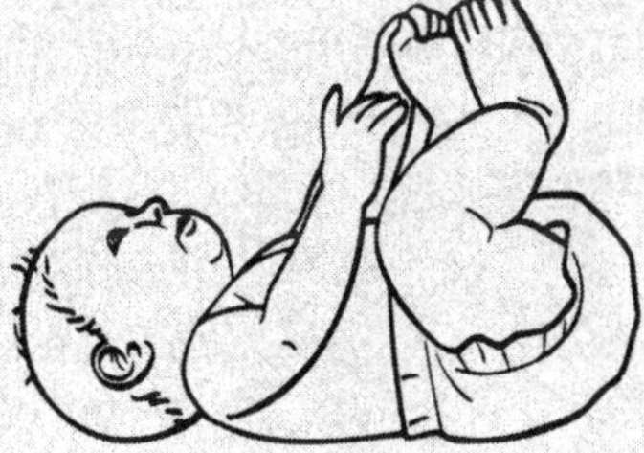

1. Peter the Wild Boy

In the summer of 1724 a peculiar youth was found in the forest of Hertswold near Hameln in northern Germany. Aged about 13, he walked on all fours and fed on grass and leaves. 'A naked, brownish, blackhaired creature', he would run up trees when approached and could utter no intelligible sound. The latest in a long line of feral children – in turn celebrated, shunned and cursed through the ages – 'The Wild Boy of Hameln' would be the first to achieve real fame.

After a spell in the House of Correction in Celle, the boy was taken to the court of George, Duke of Hanover and King of the United Kingdom, at Herrenhausen. There the young curiosity was initially treated as an honoured guest. Seated at table with the king, dressed in a suit of clothes with a napkin at his neck, he repelled his host with his complete lack of manners. He refused bread, but gorged himself on vegetables, fruit and rare meat, greedily grasping at the dishes and eating noisily from his hands, until he was ordered to be taken away. He was given the name of Peter, but was variously known as 'Wild Peter', 'Peter of Hanover', or, most famously, 'Peter the Wild Boy'.

In the spring of 1726, after briefly escaping back to the forest, Peter was brought to London where his tale had aroused particular interest. As in Hanover, he caused a sensation and his carefree nature provided an amusing antidote to the stultifying boredom and decorum of court life. He appealed especially to Caroline, Princess of Wales, who persuaded the king to allow Peter to move to her residence in the West End, where he was kept virtually as a pet. Though he insisted on sleeping on the floor, he was dressed carefully each morning in a tailor-made suit of green and red. He was also appointed a tutor, who had him baptised and taught him to bow and kiss the hands of the ladies at court.

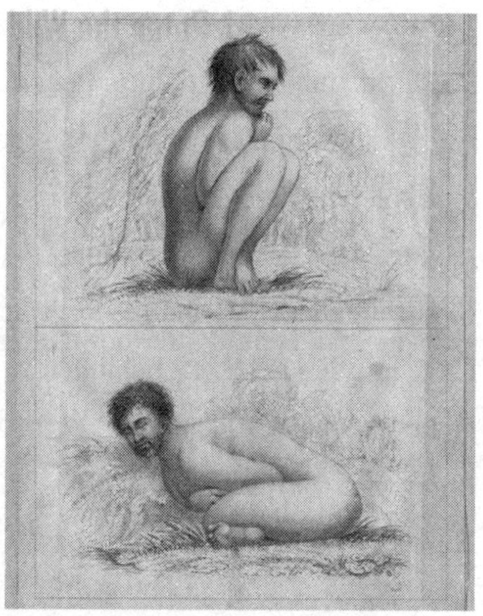

Sitting and sleeping position of Peter

Peter quickly became a celebrity. On one level, tales of his antics busied the London gazettes. Jonathan Swift, whose fictional 'Yahoos' Peter appeared to personify, noted sourly that 'there is scarcely talk of anything else'. He was soon the 'talk of the town', his portrait graced the walls of the King's Grand Staircase at Kensington Palace and an effigy of him was erected in a waxworks on the Strand. In 1727 a premature report of his death gave rise to a mocking epitaph in the British Journal. His resemblance to Swift's fantastical characters had clearly not been missed:

Ye Yahoos mourn, for in this Place

Lies dead the Glory of your Race,

One, who from Adam had Descent,

Yet ne'er did what he might repent;

But liv'd, unblemish'd, to fifteen,

And yet, O strange, a Court had seen,

Was solely rul'd by Nature's Laws,

And dy'd a Martyr in her Cause!

Now reign, ye Houynhnms, for Mankind,

Have no such Peter left behind,

None like the dear departed Youth,

Renown'd for Purity and Truth,

He was your Rival, and our Boast,

For ever, ever, ever lost!

But Peter could not to live up to the popular interest invested in him and a fickle public quickly abandoned him in favour of the next unfortunate. His academic progress also failed to match his earlier promise. He was declared 'unable to receive instruction', despite the attentions of 'the ablest masters'. He could say nothing beyond his own name and a garbled form of 'King George'. By 1728, his tutor had given up his efforts and Peter was retired to the country. A home was found for him on a farm near Northchurch in Hertfordshire and a generous crown pension of £35 per annum was supplied for his upkeep. The 'talk of the town' became a humble farm hand.

Though still only an adolescent, Peter faded into provincial obscurity and thereafter rarely troubled the gossip columns. He developed a taste for gin and loved music, reportedly swaying and clapping with glee and dancing until he was exhausted. But he never learned to speak and his lack of any sense of direction gave cause for concern. In 1745, the year of the Jacobite Rebellion, he was arrested as a suspected Highlander and, six years later, he wandered as far as Norwich, where he was thought to be a Spanish subversive. As a result he was fitted with a heavy leather collar bearing the inscription: 'Peter, the Wild Man of Hanover. Whoever will bring him to Mr Fenn at Berkhamsted, Hertfordshire, shall be paid for their trouble.' He finally died, aged around 72, in 1785.

Though Peter's life is remarkable enough, what is most astounding is the sheer scale of scientific and philosophical interest that his case aroused. While wits opined that the boy might be corrupted by the sybaritic life of London high society, others saw in him an ideal test case for the nascent sciences of anthropology and psychology.

To the thinkers of the Age of Reason, Peter represented a blank slate. As humanity in its 'raw' state, he was what Jean-Jacques Rousseau called 'the noble savage', man 'unspoilt' by society and civilisation. He was indeed a fascinating subject, but he provoked further, disquieting, enquiry. He was undoubtedly human but, lacking speech and socialisation, could he be classed as a man? Could he have a soul? Could he possess the power of thought?

Of the numerous thinkers and writers who addressed the subject, Daniel Defoe did so with the most clarity in his pamphlet *Mere Nature Delineated*, published in 1726. He described Peter as an 'object of pity' but cast doubt on the story of his origins, dismissing it as a 'Fib'. On the issue of Peter's soul, he was more charitable. Possessed of the gift of laughter and thought, Peter clearly had a soul, he wrote, but its powers did not yet act within him. He was, in sum, 'in a state of Mere Nature … a ship without a Rudder'. And it was the task of his tutors to bring him to 'the Use of his Reason'. He deferred the final verdict on Peter, therefore, until the results of his education became apparent. If he could receive instruction – if he could be taught to heed his soul – then he would become a man. And, what was more, he would be a lesson to us all, especially, wrote Defoe, 'those who think nobody so wise as themselves'.

Defoe wrestled manfully with the uncomfortable question that Peter posed: what was it that divided 'us' from 'them', man from the animals? Different minds arrived at different conclusions. But the habitual tidier of nature Carl Linnaeus was typical. He reassured mankind by creating a separate species of 'wild men' or homo ferens. Peter was still clearly an outsider – one of 'them'.

Peter's example was later used in numerous theories of child development, socialisation and the role of language. Many thinkers dwelt on his inability to learn to speak. The philosopher James Burnett (Lord Monboddo), whose ideas anticipated some of Darwin's, presented him as an illustration of his theory of the evolution of language in the human species. He saw Peter as evidence that 'man was born mute, and that articulation is altogether … a habit acquired by custom and exercise'. To others, Peter was thought to demonstrate the existence of a 'critical window' in which language and other skills are developed in the child. Having missed the 'window', Peter could never learn such skills again. Hence the apparent failure of his esteemed tutors.

Other scientists concentrated on the role of 'socialisation' in child development. After a childhood supposedly devoid of parental care and nurture, Peter was considered to have developed a 'mental indifference' and a lack of empathy, reflection and memory. In common with other feral children, it was argued, he 'lived solely to survive', satisfying only his base desires for food and sleep. In other interpretations, Peter's mental shortcomings were attributed primarily to his lack of language. Having never learned to speak, it was suggested, how could he comprehend his own 'inner voice'? How could he order and make sense of his world? The result was that he was virtually unable to display higher mental functions. He was trapped in the mind of a toddler.

The 19th-century German anthropologist Johann Friedrich Blumenbach (1752-1840) then rather spoiled the intellectual party. Examining contemporary accounts, which suggested that Peter had been tonguetied (hence his inability to speak) and had webbed fingers on one hand (a common corollary to mental impairment), he concluded that 'the Wild Boy' was most probably mentally retarded. If this was the case, he argued, it would help to explain Peter's peculiar origins – a point that had also bothered Defoe.

Rather than being a genuine 'feral child' then, Peter was most probably abandoned, possibly only weeks before his discovery. Most importantly, however, if he had been mentally disabled, then all the noble theories of development and socialisation which relied on his example were rendered lame. The 'noble savage' had been a simple charity case, worthy of pity certainly, but not philosophical enquiry.

Feral children have always aroused man's fascination. But when Peter stumbled out of the forest in 1725 he encountered a world in intellectual ferment. Inspired by the Light of Reason and the Scientific Revolution, Europe's new secular intelligentsia was examining the world anew after centuries of obscurantism and superstition. An army of frustrated empiricists, they submitted everything and everyone to rational investigation. To them, Peter was a godsend: 'the very Creature which the learned World have … pretended to wish for'. They pamphleteered, polemicised and pontificated. But, like their subject, they were stumbling into the unknown, often lacking the words to pose the right questions and the knowledge to interpret their observations correctly. As a mute, Peter was unable to disabuse them of their wilder conjectures and his mystery only deepened, fuelling the debate and spurring the theorists. In a sense, the philosophers of the Age of Reason had met their match. They were faced with a man who did not make sense. But, for all their theories, it did not occur to them that he could not make sense – that there was no 'sense' to make. As Defoe had suggested, it is quite possible that they brought 'an Idiot upon the Stage, and made a great Something out of Nothing'.

Whatever his ailments, Peter was not forgotten by the royal court. His keep was paid by the crown for nearly 60 years through three reigns and when he died a brass tablet was erected to his memory at royal expense. But Peter was no more loquacious in death than he had been in life. He was given a prime spot in the graveyard at Northchurch, close to the south porch, and his rough-hewn stone, now shaded by an unruly dog rose, reads simply: 'Peter the Wild Boy – 1785'.

■■

2. The Wild Girl of Champagne – Memmie Le Blanc

Memmie was first sighted around the village of Songi, near Chalôns, in the French district of Champagne, one September evening in 1731. She appeared from the woods armed with a club and in search of water. When one of the frightened villagers set a guard dog on her, she gave it a heavy blow on the head with her club, killing it instantly. Then, after jumping over the dead animal several times in ecstatic celebration, she climbed to the top of a tree and fell asleep.

The villagers brought the news to Viscount d'Epinoy at his chateau in Songi who, curious about the child, ordered them to try and catch her. Knowing she was thirsty they left a pitcher of water beneath the tree in which she was sleeping. As they thought, she came down and drank from the water, but, before anyone could act, she had darted back to the treetop. A woman with a child then approached the tree and stood at the bottom, hoping to make the strange girl feel less afraid. The woman smiled, acted in a friendly manner, and offered the girl vegetables and fish. But despite her obvious hunger, she only descended a part of the way, before becoming scared and scampering back to the top of the tree. The woman continued to try and coax the girl down and, eventually, the plan was successful and she slid down from her place of safety to get the food. As the girl approached the woman moved slowly away, and a group of men who'd been waiting behind some bushes seized her and took her away.

She was brought to the kitchen of the chateau of Viscount d'Epinoy, where the cook was preparing some fowls for the viscount's dinner. Suddenly, the girl rushed at the dead birds, grabbed one and began to devour it.

When d'Epinoy arrived and saw the savage child, he told the cook to give her an unskinned rabbit, which the little girl immediately skinned and ate greedily.

The villagers questioned the girl, but she couldn't understand any French; the only way she knew how to communicate was by shrieks and squeaks. At first they thought she was black, but after several hot baths which washed away the dirt – and possibly paint – they found her skin to be white. She had blue eyes and was thought to be about nine or ten years old. On further examination she was found to have unusually shaped hands, with enlarged fingers and thumbs. This was later attributed to her swinging from one tree to another, grabbing at the branches with her strong hands, and her using her thumbs to dig up roots. Her feet were bare, but she wore a tattered dress of rags and animal skins, and a gourd leaf on her hair in place of a hat. She also wore a necklace, pendants, and a pouch attached to a large animal skin wrapped around her body. Inside the pouch she carried a club, and a knife inscribed with strange characters, which nobody could decipher.

The Viscount put the wild girl in the care of a shepherd, but she frequently tried to escape, once being found in the top of a winter tree during a severe snow storm. The girl refused to sleep on a bed, preferring the floor instead, and would only eat bread and drink only water, cooked meat making her vomit (as with Kaspar Hauser). There was much conjecture about her origin, Norway was mentioned, but at the time somewhere in the West Indies was thought more likely.

Memmie ran and swam exceptionally well, had incredibly sharp eyesight, and caught and ate small animals and fish from the bottoms of rivers.

On 30 October, 1731, she was put in the charge of the hospital general at St. Maur in nearby Chalôns, though she still seems to have spent time with the shepherd at Songi or with Viscount d'Epinoy at his chateau. At first she was terrified at even being touched, and she would shriek and become wild-eyed when it happened. But gradually she became tamer and more 'civilised', and also began to progress well at learning French, indicating not only that she was fairly intelligent, but that she had been able to speak before her abandonment. Her mother tongue, however, was completely lost.

'Memmie Le Blanc'

On 16 June, 1732, the girl was baptized with the name Marie-Angélique Memmie Le Blanc. Unfortunately, despite the novel appeal of her case, captivity was detrimental to Memmie's health and spirits. The Viscount d'Epinoy had been careful to give her the raw meat and root vegetables she was used to, but the increasing amount of time she spent at the hospital at St. Maur changed this. The cooked meats, food preserved with salt, and wine provided for her at St. Maur made her teeth and nails drop out, and she was frequently in poor health. The bleedings directed by the doctors to try and lessen her savageness only made her more ill, and in combination with the new diet brought her close to death. Indeed her health was permanently ruined by this treatment.

Within a year of Memmie's capture, Viscount d'Epinoy died, and she was put in the care of the Convent des régentes at Chalôns, where she learned how to make artificial flowers and was forced to stop climbing trees and swimming. Consequently her wildness soon began to fade, though not completely.

In 1737, the Queen of Poland, mother to the French queen, heard about this strange girl when she was travelling through Champagne to take possession of the Duchy of Lorraine. The queen decided to take her hunting, where Memmie still retained enough of her wild nature that she ran fast enough to catch and kill rabbits.

Very little is known about the next ten years of Memmie's life. In September 1747, now a young woman and fluent in French, she left Chalôns for the convent at St. Menehold, in Paris, perhaps hoping to avoid attention. Here she met a Msr. La Condamine, a middle-aged aristocrat and renowned scientist. He had her moved to another Parisian convent where she prepared to become a nun. But while there one of the windows collapsed on her head and left her life in danger once again. She was taken to the house of the Hospitalières, where she obtained the best possible medical help, paid for by a rich patron, the Duke of Orléans. But circumstances were against her once more, when the Duke died and she was left alone, sick and without financial support of any kind. In this way she spent the next few years of her life.

Then, in November 1752, she met another patron, her biographer Madame Hecquet. Her biography of Memmie was published in 1755. Madame Hecquet had much difficulty getting Memmie to remember her life before the capture. The girl told her that she hadn't began to reflect on her life until after being taken (as Kaspar Hauser). She could remember no home or family, the only particular memory was of seeing a large sea animal with a round head and big eyes, that swum with two feet like a dog. Madame Hecquet thought it might be a seal and wondered if Memmie was in fact an Eskimo. But Memmie did not look at all like an Eskimo, she was fair-skinned and had softer European features.

In March 1765, still in Paris, Memmie met yet another patron, James Burnett, the future Lord Monboddo. She was unwell at the time and had tried to make a living, unsuccessfully as a public curiosity. When she met Burnett she was scraping an existence by making artificial flowers and selling her memoirs.

Memmie Relates her History

As told to Burnett, Memmie's story of her life previous to her capture at Songi is, if true, an incredible one. She thought she must have been seven or eight years old when she was carried off from her native land, the name or location of which she couldn't remember. She said she was put on board a large ship and taken on a voyage to a warm country, where she was sold into slavery. Before selling her, however, her captors had painted her entire body black, in order to pass her off as a black slave and not give rise to any suspicions about her origins.

In the same country she was put on board another ship, where the master made her do needlework, and beat her if she didn't work. Her mistress, on the other hand, was more kind-hearted and would hide her from the master. But disaster followed, the ship was wrecked and the crew took the life boat, leaving Memmie and a black girl to look after themselves. They managed to swim from the sinking ship, with the black girl, a weak swimmer, keeping herself from drowning by clutching Memmie's foot.

Finally the two girls reached shore. They then journeyed a long distance across land, travelling only at night to avoid being seen. Sleeping through the day in the tops of trees, they survived by eating roots dug out from the ground, and when they managed to, catching wild animals which they ate raw, like the beasts of the forest. Apparently Memmie learned to imitate birdsong, as that was the only kind of music known in her country. The main difficulty the two girls had was that they couldn't speak each other's language, so they only communicated by signs and wild shrieks, like those the frightened French villagers had heard when they tried to catch Memmie.

A few days before her capture, Memmie came upon a Rosary lying on the ground. Excited at the find, but also wary that her wild friend would pick it up, she reached down to take it first. But the other girl struck Memmie's hand as hard as she could with her club. Her hand was hurt badly, but she was able to strike her opponent a fierce blow on her brow, at which the girl reeled over bleeding and screaming. At this Memmie became touched with regret and rushed off to find some frogs. Finding one, she cut off its skin and placed it over the girl's forehead to stem the flow of blood from the wound, and tied the dressing in place with thread made from tree bark. After this, Memmie said, the two companions separated. The wounded girl going back towards the river, and Memmie taking the path towards Songi.

Apparently the young black girl continued to be seen in the area, around the town of Cheppe, after Memmie's capture, but was never caught, and no more was heard of her. Other reports say that Memmie actually killed the other girl accidentally in the disagreement.

There is no record of what finally became of Memmie Le Blanc, but, as with most feral children, she probably died poor and forgotten. Madame Hecquet seems to have disappeared, and what may have been vital clues to Memmie's origin, the possessions she had when captured at Songi (especially the knife with the strange inscriptions) were never found. Perhaps the truth was much more prosaic than her biography, and she was a French peasant child abandoned in the woods at an early age, and her later stories were false memories. But what of her black companion?

The possibility that Memmie was an unfortunate child caught up in the huge Atlantic slave trade of the time, where slaves were known to be painted black for easier sale, cannot be discounted; but where she came from originally will probably never be known.

■■

3. The Wild Boy of Aveyron – Victor of Aveyron

Victor of Aveyron (also The Wild Boy of Aveyron) was a feral child who apparently lived his entire childhood naked and alone in the woods before being found wandering the woods near Saint-Sernin-sur-Rance, France, in 1797. He was captured, but soon escaped after being displayed in the town. He was additionally periodically spotted in 1798 and 1799.

However, on January 8, 1800, he emerged from the forests on his own. His age was unknown, but citizens of the village estimated he was about twelve years old. His lack of speech, as well as his food preferences and the numerous scars on his body, indicated he had been in the wild for the majority of his life. While the townspeople received him kindly, it was only a matter of time before word spread and the boy was quickly taken for examination and documentation.

His case was taken up by a young physician, Jean Marc Gaspard Itard, who worked with the boy (whom he named Victor) for five years. Itard was interested in determining what Victor could learn. He devised procedures to teach the boy words and recorded his progress. Based on his work with Victor, Itard broke new ground in the education of the developmentally delayed.

Study

Shortly after Victor was found, a local abbot and biology professor, Pierre Joseph Bonnaterre, examined him. He removed the boy's clothing and led him outside into the snow, where, far from being upset, Victor began to frolic about in the nude, showing Bonnaterre that he was clearly accustomed to exposure and cold. The local government commissioner, Constans-Saint-Esteve, also observed the boy and wrote there was "something extraordinary in his behaviour, which makes him seem close to the state of wild animals". The boy was eventually taken to Rodez, where two men traveled to discover whether or not he was their missing son. Both men had lost their sons during the French Revolution, but neither claimed the boy as his son. There were other rumours regarding the boy's origins. For example, one rumour insisted the boy was the illegitimate son of a notaire abandoned at a young age because he was mute. Itard believed Victor had "lived in an absolute solitude from his fourth or fifth almost to his twelfth year, which is the age he may have been when he was taken in the Caune woods." That means he presumably lived for seven years in the wilderness.

It was clear that Victor could hear, but he was taken to the National Institute of the Deaf in Paris for the purpose of being studied by the renowned Roch-Ambroise Cucurron Sicard. Sicard and other members of the Society of Observers of Man believed that by studying, as well as educating the boy, they would gain the proof they needed for the recently popularized empiricist theory of knowledge. In the context of the Enlightenment, when many were debating what exactly distinguished man from animal, one of the most significant factors was the ability to learn language. By studying the boy, they would also be able to explain the relationship between man and society.

Influence of the Enlightenment

The Enlightenment caused many thinkers, including naturalists and philosophers, to believe human nature was a subject that needed to be redefined and looked at from a completely different angle. Because of the French Revolution and new developments in science and philosophy, man was looked at as not special, but as characteristic of his place in nature. It was hoped that by studying the wild boy, this idea would gain support. He became a case study in the Enlightenment debate about the differences between humans and other animals.

At that time, the scientific category Juvenis averionensis was used, as a special case of the Homo ferus, described by Carl von Linné in Systema Naturae. Linnaeus and his discoveries, then, forced people to ask the question, what makes us men? Another developing idea that was prevalent during the Enlightenment was the idea of the noble savage. Some believed a man, existing in the pure state of nature, would be "gentle, innocent, a lover of solitude, ignorant of evil and incapable of causing intentional harm."

Philosophies proposed by the likes of Rousseau, Locke, and Descartes were evolving around the time when the boy was discovered in France in 1800. These advances in philosophy invariably had an influence on how the boy was looked at, and eventually, how his education would be constructed by Itard.

Influence of Colonialism

Simpson points out there was a "direct link between the discourse of colonialism abroad and internal regulation of deviants back home." The same way in which Europeans viewed the "Other" in colonies and other exotic locations was how the French people saw the Wild Boy of Aveyron. To lack reason and understanding during the Enlightenment was to be uncivilized. The attitudes that Europeans extended toward the Other were paralleled by Victor, as he too was considered "uncivilized" because of his lack of language and therefore, reason. These characteristics defined mankind for Victor's contemporaries.

Education

After Sicard became frustrated with the lack of progress made by the boy, he was left to roam the institution by himself, until Itard decided to take the boy into his home to keep reports and monitor his development. However, it was said that even though he had been exposed to society and education, he had made little progress at the Institution under Sicard. Many people questioned his ability to learn because of his initial state, and as

Yousef explains, "it is one thing to say that the man of nature is not yet fully human; it is quite another thing to say that the man of nature cannot become fully human."

Jean Marc Gaspard Itard

Jean Marc Gaspard Itard, a young medical student, effectively adopted Victor into his home and published reports on his progress. Itard believed two things separated humans from animals: empathy and language. He wanted to civilize Victor with the objectives of teaching him to speak and to communicate human emotion. Victor showed significant early progress in understanding language and reading simple words, but failed to progress beyond a rudimentary level. Itard wrote, "Under these circumstances his ear was not an organ for the appreciation of sounds, their articulations and their combinations; it was nothing but a simple means of self-preservation which warned of the approach of a dangerous animal or the fall of wild fruit."

The only two phrases Victor ever actually learned to spell out were lait (milk) and Oh, Dieu (Oh, God). It would seem, however, that Itard implemented more contemporary views when he was educating Victor. Rousseau appears to have believed "that natural association is based on reciprocally free and equal respect between people." [10] This notion of how to educate and to teach was something that although did not produce the effects hoped for, did prove to be a step towards new systems of pedagogy. By attempting to learn about the boy who lived in nature, education could be restructured and characterized.

Itard has been recognized as the founder of "oral education of the deaf; the field of Otolaryngology; the use of behaviour modification with severely impaired children; and special education for the mentally and physically handicapped."

While Victor did not learn to speak the language that Itard tried to teach him, it seems that Victor did make progress in his behaviour towards other people. At the Itard home, housekeeper Madame Guérin was setting the table one evening while crying over the loss of her husband. Victor stopped what he was doing and displayed consoling behaviour towards her. Itard reported on this progress.

Language

When looking at the association between language and intellect, French society considered one with the other. Unless cared for by friends or family, most people considered "dumb" ended up in horrible, ghastly conditions. However, around 1750, something different was happening in Paris. A French priest, Charles-Michel de l'Épée, created a school to educate deaf-mutes. His institution was made into a National Institute in 1790. This new interest and moral obligation towards deaf-mutes inspired Itard to nurture and attempt to teach Victor language. "He had Locke's and Condiallac's theory that we are born with empty heads and that our ideas arise from what we perceive and experience. Having experienced almost nothing of society, the boy remained a savage."

Throughout the years Itard spent working with Victor, he made some gradual progress. Victor understood the meaning of actions and used what Shattuck describes as "action language", which Itard regarded as a kind of primitive form of communication. However, Itard still could not get Victor to speak. He wondered why Victor would choose to remain mute when he had already proved that he was not, in fact, deaf. Victor also did not understand tones of voice. Itard proclaimed "Victor was the mental and psychological equivalent of a born deaf-mute. There would be little point in trying to teach him to speak by the normal means of repeating sounds if he didn't really hear them."

Shattuck critiques Itard's process of education, wondering why he never attempted to teach Victor to use sign language.

Regardless, today there are certain hypotheses that Shattuck applies to Victor. "One is that the Wild Boy, though born normal, developed a serious mental or psychological disturbance before his abandonment. Precocious schizophrenia, infantile psychosis, autism—a number of technical terms have been applied to his position. Several psychiatrists I have consulted favour this approach. It provides both a motivation for abandonment and an explanation for his partial recovery under Itard's treatment."

Victor died in Paris in 1828 in the home of Madame Guérin.

■ ■

4. Kaspar Hauser – Wild Child of Europe

The 26th May, 1828, was a major holiday and the streets of Nuremberg were almost empty. Between four and five o'clock in the afternoon, Georg Weickmann, a shoemaker who lived in Unschlitt Square, noticed a strange boy of between fifteen and eighteen years old, dressed in coarse peasant clothes and walking strangely as if drunk. The shoemaker approached him and the boy held out a sealed envelope addressed 'To the Honourable Captain of the Cavalry of the Fourth Squadron, of the Sixth Regiment of the Light Cavalry in Nuremberg.' On seeing the address Weickmann took the stranger to the Guard Tower in front of the New Gate, to find out where the captain lived, and then on to the captain's house.

When they arrived at the address, they found that the captain was not home, and were asked to wait. The servants offered them food and drink, but the boy spat out the beer and sausage given to him as if he'd never tasted such things before. In the end he accepted a meal of plain black bread and water, and ate as if starved, though he didn't seem to know how to use his fingers properly. The boy appeared to be in extreme pain and wept continually, pointing to his feet. Weickmann and the servants tried to talk to him, but the only answers they got were 'I don't know', and 'I would like to be a rider the way my father was.' Finally, thinking him some sort of wild man, they put him in the stable, where he immediately fell asleep.

When Captain Wessenig arrived home, he was told the news of the strange visitor and demanded to see him at once. There was some difficulty in waking the boy from his deep sleep, and, when he finally awoke, he was spellbound at the captain's uniform. But like everyone else the captain could get no sense from the boy, and, thinking there was nothing he could do, sent him to the police station.

At the station the police questioned the young stranger again, but all they got was the same 'don't know' or 'take me home!' He showed practically no reaction to anything, behaving as if in a trance, and was perfectly happy when a policeman gave him a coin to play with, saying 'Horse! Horse!' One of the policemen then had the idea of giving him a pen, ink and paper and telling him to write. To everyone's surprise he wrote the name Kaspar Hauser, 'in firm, legible letters.'

Kaspar was about four feet nine inches tall, had light brown curly hair, and was stocky with broad shoulders. His skin was very fair and delicate, though he didn't have a sickly complexion, his hands were small and soft, and his blistered feet showed no signs of ever having worn shoes. He had a wound on his right arm and, according to some sources, also a vaccination mark, probably suggesting an upper-class origin.

He was wearing a round felt peasant's hat lined with yellow silk, an old pair of high-heeled half boots that didn't fit, a black silk scarf, a gray cloth jacket, a linen vest, and gray cloth trousers. He was carrying a white and red checked handkerchief with the initials K.H. embroidered in red, and some rags decorated with blue and white flowers, a (possibly) German key, a small envelope containing gold dust (!), and prayer beads made of horn. He also had some printed religious texts in his pockets, including a spiritual manual entitled '*The Art of Replacing Lost Time and Years Badly Spent*', a cynical title in view of what was later found out about his history.

Confinement in the Tower

Kaspar was soon handed over to a policeman and locked in the upper floor of Vetsner Gate tower, under the guard of a sympathetic and inquisitive jailer, Andreas Hiltel. To make sure there was no deception on Kaspar's part, a physician was ordered to monitor the boy and the jailer was to observe him secretly. Hiltel's eleven year-old son and three year old daughter became good friends with Kaspar, and the son taught him the alphabet and how to draw, and 'virtually taught him to speak' in the words of the jailer.

After a few days Kaspar was moved to the lower floor of the tower where the jailer and his family lived. Here the jailer soon noticed some strange things about the boy. His facial expressions were limited to an innocent smile, and he was not embarrassed at being bathed by the jailer and his wife, seeming not to understand the differences between the sexes. He later said he told the difference between men and women by the kinds of clothes they wore. The boy seemed perfectly happy to sit alone in his cell motionless and mute, with his legs stretched out in front of him. When he did attempt to walk he was unsteady on his feet, like a small child learning to take its first steps.

The letters Hauser was carrying were examined by the authorities. One letter was 'From the boarder of Bavaria', and written in simulated Bavarian dialect. It stated that the writer was sending the captain a boy who would like to faithfully serve his king in the army. The boy had been left with the writer, 'a poor day labourer', on 7 October, 1812. The boy's mother had asked the labourer to bring the boy up, but with ten children of his own, he already had enough to do. The letter went on to say that the boy had always been confined to the house, and that if the boy's parents had lived, he might have had the chance of a good education, as he was a quick learner and could do anything after being shown once. The labourer also said that he had already taught the boy to read and write and that 'he writes my handwriting exactly as I do.' It finished strangely and menacingly:

'If you can't keep him, you will have to butcher him or hang him up in the chimney.' It was unsigned, but dated 1828.

The second letter, apparently the one given to the poor labourer along with Kaspar, was dated 1812, and claimed to have been written by the boy's mother. It said that the child had been born on 30 April,1812, and baptised Kaspar, but the labourer should give him a second name himself. Kaspar's father was dead, apparently, and had been a cavalry soldier, so when the boy was seventeen the labourer was to take him to Nuremberg to the Sixth Cavalry regiment – which his father had belonged to. The writer was 'a poor little girl' who couldn't feed the boy.

When the letters were studied closely, it was discovered that they were probably written by the same hand, with the same ink and on the same kind of paper.

Kaspar was unhappy at first in his strange new environment, and cried frequently for the first week or so. A royal forensic physician's diagnosis was that the boy was not insane or dull-witted, but had been forcibly removed from all human and social education. He also noted an abnormality of the bone structure of his knees, perhaps from only rarely having stood up. It was also noticed that Kaspar was far more comfortable at night and was even able to see in the dark. This all seemed to prove what the letter had said, that most of Kaspar's life had been spent confined indoors with very little, if any, contact with other people or with the outside world.

His diet continued to consist of water and black bread, as he was unable to stomach anything else. Other things about the boy attracted attention. He was always very gentle, kind and completely trusting, and could not bear harm coming to even the smallest insect. His reactions were as if he was seeing life for the first time. Delighted at the bright light of a candle, he burnt his hand when he attempted to touch the flame, and began to scream and cry in pain. When a mirror was put in front of him, he tried to touch his own reflection and looked behind it to find the person he believed was hiding there. Any shiny object would grab his attention and he cried like a baby when he wasn't allowed to have it.

At first Kaspar had no conception of humans or animals; he knew of nothing apart from 'boys', meaning himself and the man who'd always been with him, and 'horse', the toy he'd played with. He called all animals 'horse', but, although he liked light coloured animals, he was very afraid of dark colours. In the tower he was given some toy horses, which he became very attached to and played with for hours in his room, taking no notice of what went on around him.

Soon, however, he began to tire of these inanimate toys and started to draw, hanging the pictures on the walls of his small room.

Public interest in the mysterious youth grew daily and crowds assembled to gaze as he ate and slept. Many thought, since he could hardly walk, could speak only a few strange sentences, and was able to hear but not understand what was said to him, that he must be a feral child.

Kaspar's Past Life

As Kaspar's vocabulary grew details of his disturbing past life emerged. In his Autobiography, written in 1829 (published in Jeffrey Moussaieff Masson's book – *Lost Prince: The Unsolved Mystery of Kaspar Hauser*), he writes that he had grown up in a tiny 'cage' 6 or 7ft long, 4ft wide and only 5ft high. With the two windows boarded up, there was hardly any light, and he never saw the sun. The ceiling consisted of two large pieces of wood, pushed and tied together. He was never allowed out, and the entrance was guarded by a low locked door. He had a straw bed to sleep on a dirt floor, and a woollen blanket, and there was a round hole or bucket where he could relieve himself. He never saw his jailer as he always approached him from behind in the darkness, insisting Kaspar's back was turned. According to Hauser, he never slept lying down, but rather sitting with his back vertical and his legs straight out in front. Each morning he found a jug of water and a piece of bread at his side; sometimes the water had a bitter taste and sent him to sleep, and he awoke to find his clothes had been changed and his hair and nails cut. On these occasions the water probably contained opium;

Hauser later confirmed this when a drop was put in water by his doctor for him to drink, and he said it tasted just like the water in his cage.

While imprisoned he was given two white wooden horses, a wooden dog, and some red ribbons to play with. Like a young child he believed the animals to be alive and talked to them as if this was the case. Even after months in Nuremberg he did not understand that these animals were not real. He never saw any other human beings or heard any sounds of life while imprisoned. But he said he was never sick and only felt pain once, when he made too much noise and his jailer hit him with a stick. The scars from this blow on his right elbow were still there when he was examined in Nuremberg.

There are problems with Kaspar's story. Its difficult to believe someone could survive on such a diet of bread and water for any length of time, unless of course he wasn't kept imprisoned for anywhere near the length of time people later thought. He himself had no idea how long he was in the cage, or indeed of time in general. But he said he was always content because nobody hurt him.

One day, the jailor, whom Kaspar called 'the man', came into his cell barefoot and poorly dressed. He gave Kaspar some books and told him he must learn to read and write, and go to his father who was a rider, and then he too would become a rider. Kaspar learnt how to read a little, to write his name, and say 'I want to be a soldier as my father was.' He was also taught how to stand up, and warned never to try and get out of the door of his room, as God would be angry and punish him.

One night, the man appeared and told him he was going to take him away. Kaspar didn't want to go but was again persuaded with promises of seeing his father and becoming a rider as he was. The man lifted Kaspar onto his back and carried him outside, and they travelled until daybreak. Kasper, assaulted by the light and the new smells, fainted, or was given opium again to make him sleep as he travelled.

Later on the man put Kaspar down, and taught him to walk, which was difficult for him as he was barefoot and his feet were tender. On the third day the man made Kaspar change clothes and taught him a couple of prayers, and once again told him he would be a rider like his father. The food they ate on the journey was bread and water, as in his prison. Hauser was told to look only at the ground while he walked so as to keep from falling, this meant that he didn't see the surroundings as they travelled. As they drew near to Nuremberg, which the man called the 'big village', Kaspar was given the letter for the captain and told to go to the big village, the man saying he'd follow later.

So Kaspar walked on alone into Nuremberg and finally arrived at the gate where he met the shoemaker.

Daumer's Guardianship

Among the visitors who flocked to see Kaspar was the famous magistrate and criminologist Anselm Ritter von Feuerbach. He visited him in on 11 June, 1828, and noted Kaspar's fondness for bright and shiny objects, especially women's clothes and soldier's uniforms, and also his sensitivity to light. He also noted that there was no movement of the boy's facial muscles, and that his eyes stared blankly into space. At that time Kaspar could only make himself understood with difficulty and always spoke of himself in the third person – 'Kasper very good' rather than 'I am very good', and spoke to people in the third person –'Mister Colonel' for example, rather than saying 'you'.

The authority's investigations into Kaspar drew a blank; no one knew who he was or where he'd come from. The boy himself was not well physically, and was often depressed by the numerous visitors and new sensations he was bombarded with. Feuerbach felt Kaspar would die or go insane if he remained in the tower, so together with the Mayor, Binder, they decided that Hauser needed a guardian and a family. So, on 18 July, 1828, he was placed in the care of a university professor – George Friedrich Daumer, who had a reputation for his work in education and philosophy, and had been impressed with Hauser when he visited him two weeks after his arrival. Daumer studied Kaspar and kept a diary of the time he spent with him.

By August 1828 Kaspar had adjusted somewhat, he could express himself and make himself understood, and he could now tell the difference between living and lifeless, organic and inorganic things. Under Daumer's guidance Kaspar developed into a healthy, intelligent, and in many ways normal young man, who quickly learned the German language, though he always spoke it with a foreign accent. He also developed a sense of humour and wrote letters and essays, and mastered the art of riding a horse within a few days, riding for hours without stopping, to the wonder of the local cavalry.

Kaspar still had many peculiarities. He was sensitive to colours, his favourite being red, especially bright red, he disliked black and green and had little interest in nature because of this. In fact he disliked the view of trees and plants at Daumer's house, though he was upset when a boy hit a tree with a stick thinking it was hurt. But he was capable of amazement at nature – the first time he saw the star-filled night sky he was enraptured.

By September, he had developed psychologically enough to be curious about his former mental state; he could not imagine how he could not have wondered, when in his prison, about other living beings and life in the world outside the cage, or even where the bread and water came from. He began writing his autobiography, and this was news enough to be announced in several newspapers. He also began to eat meat for the first time and his strength gradually improved.

It was the opinion of those who met him that Kaspar was remembering language rather than learning it for the first time, so it was surmised that he must have been imprisoned somewhere between the ages of two and four.

Daumer learnt a lot more about Kaspar's extraordinary abilities, developed as the result of being brought up under such abnormal conditions. The boy proved to have extraordinarily developed senses. His sight and hearing were unusually acute, and he could hear a whisper from across the room. He could see in the dark, and demonstrated this by reading aloud from the Bible in total blackness, and he distinguished colours, even dark colours such as blue and green, in the dark. At dusk he could already recognise the constellations in the sky when a normally sharp sighted person could only distinguish a few stars.

But there was a negative side to this. Any loud sounds would cause him convulsions, and bright light caused him extreme pain. The smell of coffee, beer or any other strong drink in the same room, would make him vomit, and the smell of wine was enough to make him drunk. Apart from the few smells he was used to, most smells were repulsive to him, especially tobacco and flowers. So sharp was this sense of smell that he could identify trees by the scent of a leaf, and different people by their individual scent in the dark. He also had a photographic memory which helped him in learning to read, write and draw and play the piano.

More peculiar was his extraordinary sensitivity to electricity and metals. He would suffer extreme pain during a thunderstorm because of the static electricity in the air. Dr Daumer also discovered that Kaspar was able to distinguish between various metals merely by holding his hands above the cloth that covered them, he did this by identifying the various strengths with which the metals 'pulled' at his fingertips. In the autumn of 1828, after visiting a warehouse filled with metal, Kaspar rushed out saying that the metal had been pulling on his body from all sides.

Magnets also caused strong responses in him, the north and south poles giving him distinctly different feelings as well as different colours. When Daumer pointed the positive side of a magnet at him he clasped his chest and pulled out his vest saying 'It is dragging me, there is a draught coming out of me.' Though the negative part of the magnet had less of an effect, it still caused a reaction in him, he said it was blowing on him. However, towards the end of December 1828, this sensitivity to metal gradually disappeared, as did his other unusual attributes, as he acquired more 'practical' knowledge of the world.

By now Kaspar's extraordinary story had made him famous not only throughout the city but across Europe, and he became affectionately known as 'The Child of Europe'. He had hundreds of visitors – lawyers, doctors, teachers, public officials – and many were sure he was someone unique; articles were published about him and speculations about his origins were rife.

First Assassination Attempt

Whether it was because newspapers carried reports of Hauser's autobiography, which he would proudly show to his visitors, or because he was becoming a public figure across Europe, on Sunday 17 October 1829, while Daumer was out walking, a stranger dressed in black entered a small outhouse at Daumer's house where the boy was sitting alone, and attacked him with a butcher's knife, wounding him in the forehead. The blow was probably aimed at the throat, but Kaspar ducked and diverted it. He then fainted, and was later found lying unconscious in the cellar, where he had hidden from the man in case he returned. While in delirium after the attack Kaspar muttered in broken sentence: 'Why you kill me? I never did you anything. Not kill me! I beg not to be locked up. Never let me out of my prison – not kill me! You kill me before I understand what life is. You must tell me why you locked me up!'

Soon he managed to recover, and said that his attacker had been wearing a black silk scarf covering his whole head, and a black hat. He later told the police that the man had told him 'You must die before you leave the city of Nuremberg.' He said it was the low, quiet voice of the man who'd kept him imprisoned.

The same well dressed man was apparently seen washing his hands in a water trough not far from Daumer's house. About four days after the attack, a man answering Kaspar's description of his attacker impatiently asked a woman in the town about the condition of Hauser; he then read an official notice of the crime on the town gate, and quickly departed.

Five days after the attempted murder, shortly after the death of the reigning Grand Duke of Baden, a wealthy English aristocrat, Philip Henry – Lord Stanhope, a friend of the Baden family, arrived in Nuremberg. It seems he tried to visit Hauser but it was not possible. Behind the scenes Stanhope was gathering all the information he could on the boy.

The news of the attack soon spread and caused an uproar. Some people asserted that it must have been an assassination attempt, probably organised by the Duke of Baden, according to some Kaspar's real father, and that Kaspar was the rightful prince of Baden. But though the police organised a thorough search, no assailant was ever discovered to fit the description.

However, for many people the initial novelty of having the strange boy amongst them, and paying for his upkeep, was wearing off. It was even suggested that there had never been an attacker, and that the boy had inflicted the wounds himself and made up the story to gain attention. But the attack had a very damaging effect on Kaspar's psychology, and the wonder for the world gradually left him. The town council decided that there was a serious threat to his life, and he was moved, in January 1830, from the care of Professor Daumer's, who had by now become ill, to the care of a wealthy businessman Herr

Bieberbach, where two policemen were assigned to guard him. But there were problems between Frau Bieberbach and Kaspar, putting the boy into even more emotional confusion, and he was not happy there. Six months later he was moved again, this time into the care of Baron Von Tucher, his legal guardian, who did a great deal to restore the boy's emotional and physical health.

Lord Stanhope

In May 1831, Stanhope returned and began to visit Kaspar regularly. He showered him with gifts and compliments about his supposed royal parents, and publicly made extravagant promises about taking him to England, to his home at Chevening Castle, Kent. Unfortunately, this had the effect of cutting Kaspar off from Tucher and other people who really wanted to help him. Soon Stanhope and Hauser became close friends, and the English Lord provided money to the city for the upkeep of the boy. He also applied to the city authorities to become the boy's guardian, and the request was granted. One peculiarity of Stanhope's intense interest in Hauser is that he never once mentions him in his letters home to his family of this period, of which there are many.

But Stanhope soon became bored of Kaspar, and on 10 December 1831, obtained permission to leave him in the town of Ansbach, about fifty miles away from Nuremberg, to be tutored by his friend Dr Meyer. Kaspar was unhappy and lonely in Ansbach, Meyer was mean-minded and distrustful, a strict schoolmaster who shouted at him for not concentrating on his lessons, and told him constantly that he was telling lies.

Meyer was determined to make Kaspar into a devout Christian and threatened him with damnation if he didn't follow his religion. After a while Kaspar relented and was confirmed in the Christian faith by Pastor Fuhrmann. Stanhope left Ansbach on 9 January 1832, promising to adopt Kaspar and bring him over to England. But they never saw each other again. Stanhope actually went to see Stephanie, the Grand Duchess of Baden, at Mannheim. He gave her a copy of the just published book about Hauser by Feuerbach. She wept when she read it and was desperate to meet Hauser. Stanhope said he would arrange for them to meet, but he never did.

While staying with Meyer Hauser began working as a copying clerk in a law office. On December 9 Meyer and Hauser had a big argument, Meyer saying that Kaspar had been behaving oddly the whole of December. On 11 December Kaspar said he had to meet a friend to watch the boring of the artesian well in the park, the gardens of the disused palace.

The Assassination

On the afternoon of 14 December, Kaspar left his work at noon, and after lunch went to his spiritual guide Pastor Fuhrmann. He told Fuhrmann that he was meeting a young lady friend, but instead went to the park. Hauser later said he was tricked into going alone to the deserted gardens with the promise of information about his mother. He waited by the artesian well, but no one came, so he went across to a monument in the park, where a man was waiting for him. They walked together in the freezing cold for a while, then the man made as if to give Hauser a document and suddenly stabbed him in the side, puncturing his lung and piercing his liver, and then ran off. Kaspar managed to stagger into the house saying 'man . . . stabbed . . . knife . . . Hofgarten . . . gave purse . . . Go look quickly . . .' But Meyer was not convinced of the seriousness of the wound and did not call a doctor immediately.

Later the police searched the park but couldn't find the weapon, but did find a black wallet or purse. Inside the wallet there was a note written in mirror writing. It said:

'Hauser will be able to tell you how I look, where I came from and who I am. To spare him from this task I will tell you myself. I am from . . . on the Bavarian border . . . My name is MLO.'

Police questioned Hauser, wondering why, when there had been a previous attempt on his life, he had gone to the gardens alone. Kaspar couldn't identify his attacker, all he could tell them was that a workman had brought him a message which told him to go to the park as someone had news about his mother. When he got there, a tall, bearded man in a long, black cloak had asked him if his name was Kaspar Hauser. When Kaspar nodded, the stranger handed him the wallet or purse and thrust a knife into his ribs at the same time. As Kaspar lay dying he said, enigmatically: 'Many cats are the death of the mouse,' and finally: 'Tired, very tired, still have to take a long trip.'

He died on 17 December, at 21 years of age. A huge reward was offered by the king of Bavaria for information leading to the arrest of his killer, but nothing was ever found out.

Meyer had always been suspicious about Kaspar and it seems to have been him who started the rumours about Hauser's death being suicide. Soon others began to suspect Kaspar's story. Only a single set of footprints was found in the snow at the park, and they were Kaspar's; people suggested that Hauser may have stabbed himself in a despairing cry for attention. Stanhope later said, in his book written three years after Hauser's death, that it was accidental suicide, and that Kaspar was an imposter who got trapped in the role and was forced to keep it up for years, and made comparisons with the English impostor princess, Caraboo. But the physician who performed the autopsy, Dr. Friedrich Wilhelm Heidenreich, thought that due to the size of the wound, Kaspar could not have done it himself.

Strangely, Stanhope had actually written a last letter to Hauser, from Munich on 16th and 17th December, and postmarked on the 25th, when he must already have known of what had happened, and probably also knew that Kaspar was dead. Local newspapers carried the story from the day of Kaspar's death on the 17th, and the Munich newspapers from the 20th onwards. Was he trying to show, if questioned later, that he wasn't involved in the murder?

On 26th December Stanhope visited the prince of Öttingen-Wallerstein, Bavarian minister of the interior, and tried, unsuccessfully in the end, to convince him Hauser was a fake. He also went to the trouble of meeting with all of the people in Nuremberg who had seen Kaspar in his first few days in the city, including Daumer, and getting them to change their stories to say that Hauser had invented the whole thing. He also visited other public figures throughout Europe saying Hauser was a fake who'd committed suicide.

Kaspar was buried in a quiet country churchyard where his gravestone read:

'Here lies Kaspar Hauser, riddle of his time. His birth was unknown, his death mysterious.'

A Prince of Baden?

But who was the mysterious Kaspar Hauser? Was he the rightful prince of Baden?

It was Feuerbach who was officially in charge of the investigation into the first murder attempt. He was initially skeptical of royal claims, but later changed his mind and argued that Hauser was indeed the legitimate heir of the Duke of Baden, son of Stéphanie de Beauharnais, adopted daughter of Napoleon. He later presented the results of his investigations in a private letter to the queen mother of Bavaria, Karoline. This was published after his death by his son, but was still subject to a restraining order by the Baden family. Karoline herself stated that it was the 'unanimous opinion of many people (that) Hauser was one of the sons of my poor brother.' King Ludwig of Bavaria notes in his diary that he believed Hauser to be the 'rightful Grand Duke of Baden.' Indeed Mayor Binder had received a letter to this effect as early as July 1828.

A May 1832 letter from Feuerbach to Stanhope mentions proof about Hauser's royalty in the form of an 8 page report. It was unfortunate that the letter was to Stanhope, the one person Feuerbach trusted that he probably shouldn't have.

Feuerbach's book about Hauser caused a sensation when it was published in 1832, and newspapers all over Europe published accounts of Kaspar Hauser's life and possible origins.

However, on May 29,1832, on his way to meet a man called Klüber in Frankfurt to discuss the matter of Hauser's royal connections, Feuerbach died suddenly, aged fifty-eight. Before dying he said he thought he'd been poisoned on the orders of someone in the royal house of Baden, because of his discoveries about Hauser's origins. His son Ludwig was sure of this. There was even supposed to be a note that he wrote saying that he had been 'given something.' It was believed by Feuerbach's grandson that at least three members of the Feuerbach family were poisoned because of links to Kasper Hauser.

The 'prince theory', in essence, is that the son Stéphanie de Beauharnais, wife of Grand Duke Karl of Baden, gave birth to in 1812 was Hauser, and it is he who would have inherited the throne. She gave birth to another son in 1816, who also died. But she had three daughters that all lived. The countess of Hochberg, second wife of Karl's father, the founder of the dynasty, would have been the one to benefit from these deaths. Karl himself died in 1818, under mysterious circumstances believing he and his sons had been poisoned. Now nothing stood in the way of the son of the Duchess of Hochberg, who was supposed to have smuggled a dying child of a peasant woman into the palace and managed to exchange it with the baby prince – supposedly Kaspar Hauser. The countess wanted her own son, Leopold, to come to the throne, which he did in 1830. Hauser was then given to a Major Hennenhofer, who put the child in the care of an ex soldier. It was said by some that when questioned about this Hennenhofer confessed.

Apparently Kaspar was kept hidden away in a dungeon for twelve years. He was supposed to be killed, but the plan went wrong, and he was kept alive in prison by whoever had been ordered to murder him, possibly in order to bribe the royals later on, or perhaps out of sheer compassion. When the secret couldn't be kept hidden any longer, Hauser had to be brought disguised as a beggar to Nuremberg. Perhaps they hoped he'd be put in a lunatic asylum or sent away as a soldier.

It's possible that the place where Kaspar Hauser was imprisoned was the Schloss Pilsach, a large house close to Nuremberg, where there was a secret dungeon, and a small white wooden horse like the ones Hauser played with was discovered during renovations.

Admittedly, much evidence, the frequent attempts on Kaspar's life, the participation of Stanhope, and the Baden family's attempts to keep the story quiet, seem to indicate some truth to this prince story. Unfortunately when Hennenhofer died, his private papers were all destroyed, so that avenue, as with many in the story of Kaspar Hauser, is closed.

If the prince theory all sounds a bit too much like a fairytale, and if Hauser's death was not the accidental suicide of a desperate impostor, perhaps he could have been murdered, not for being a lost prince of the house of Baden, but because people thought he was - and he thus became a dangerous focus for discontent that needed to be removed.

Although, according to Jeffrey Moussaieff Masson (*Lost Prince: The Unsolved Mystery of Kaspar Hauser*. The Free Press, New York, 1996), there have been more than 3000 books and at least 14,000 articles written on Kaspar Hauser, the mystery still seems as far as ever from being solved.

■ ■

5. Ramchandra / Kuano – The River Boy

The village of Baragdava stands on the small river Kuano in the Basti district of Uttar Pradesh in northern India, near the border with Nepal. One afternoon in February 1973, the local priest was walking across the nearby dam across the Kuano when he caught sight of a naked boy loping towards the water. He appeared to walk out on the water to mid-stream. Suddenly he dived in and emerged a minute later with a large fish which he ate, before floating downstream. The priest told the villagers of his sighting, and when he described the lad and estimated that he was about 15, an old woman called Somni said he was her son Ramchandra who had been carried away by the river when he was a year old.

Another villager saw him a few days later, and for a while there was considerable local interest, and people flocked to the river to see him; but he was not to be found. Then in May 1979, Somni spotted him lying in a field. She crept up on him and recognised a birthmark on his back. He awoke and fled. A strict watch was mounted, he was caught and taken to the village.

He was virtually hairless and his ebony-black skin had a greenish tinge. He managed to escape back to the river, but his experience of human society made him less reclusive, and he would come and eat bowls of spinach in water put out for him. Hundreds of villagers, policemen, officials of the irrigation department, and hard-boiled journalists saw him walk, run, or recline on the surface of the water, and stay submerged for longer than ordinary humans could manage. Among the witnesses was Nazir Malik, who wrote up the story for the Allahabad magazine, *Probe India.*

The boy's insteps and toes were very hard and walked with a clumsy, loping gait, often holding one hand to his forehead. He was unable to speak (or hear, according to some witnesses). He ate fish, frogs and other marine creatures, raw meat, leafy vegetables, gourds and red chillies. He reached for food directly with his mouth. In summer months when Kuano dried to a trickle, he was ill at ease; but when the river rose in floods, he was gleeful and enjoyed diving in the swift current. It was a mystery how he avoided the jaws of the many crocodiles.

Somni had a strange tale of how Ramchandra was conceived. On a stormy evening during the monsoon season, she was returning from mending a fence around the family field, as her husband was laid low with fever. She was 40 years old, a mother of three. Her way was blocked by an enormous being who seemed more like a spirit than a man. He threw her to the ground and raped her in the pouring rain. As suddenly as he appeared, he vanished.

It was believed locally that a long time ago a holy man dug a well in the area. He climbed down to invoke the goddess of water, but was drowned as the well quickly filled. Some of the villagers believed it was the spirit of this man that possessed Somni and then took the child into his watery care.

In 1985, Hubert Adamson, an estate agent in Hampstead with a keen interest in feral children, visited Baragdava to find out more about the river boy. From the head man he learned that the boy was dead. One evening in 1982, at the age of about 24, he had approached a chai shop in the village of Sanrigar, some 300 yards from the river. A woman, possibly taking fright at his appearance or rejecting a clumsy sexual advance, threw boiling water over him. Dazed and in pain, he ran back to the river, never to emerge again. His body, badly blistered and mutilated by fish bites, was later found in the river. The police considered bringing charges against the woman, but these were later dropped.

■ ■